LISTEN, THE DRUM!

Young Matt Burnett joins the militia in this historical novel of the American Colonies just before the Revolutionary War. Soon Matt finds himself directly involved with his commander, George Washington, in an Indian-and-spy thriller. The adventures of Matt, his many companions and his few enemies are intertwined in an authentic and historically accurate dramatization of Washington's first command, the defense of Fort Necessity during the French and Indian Wars.

LISTEN

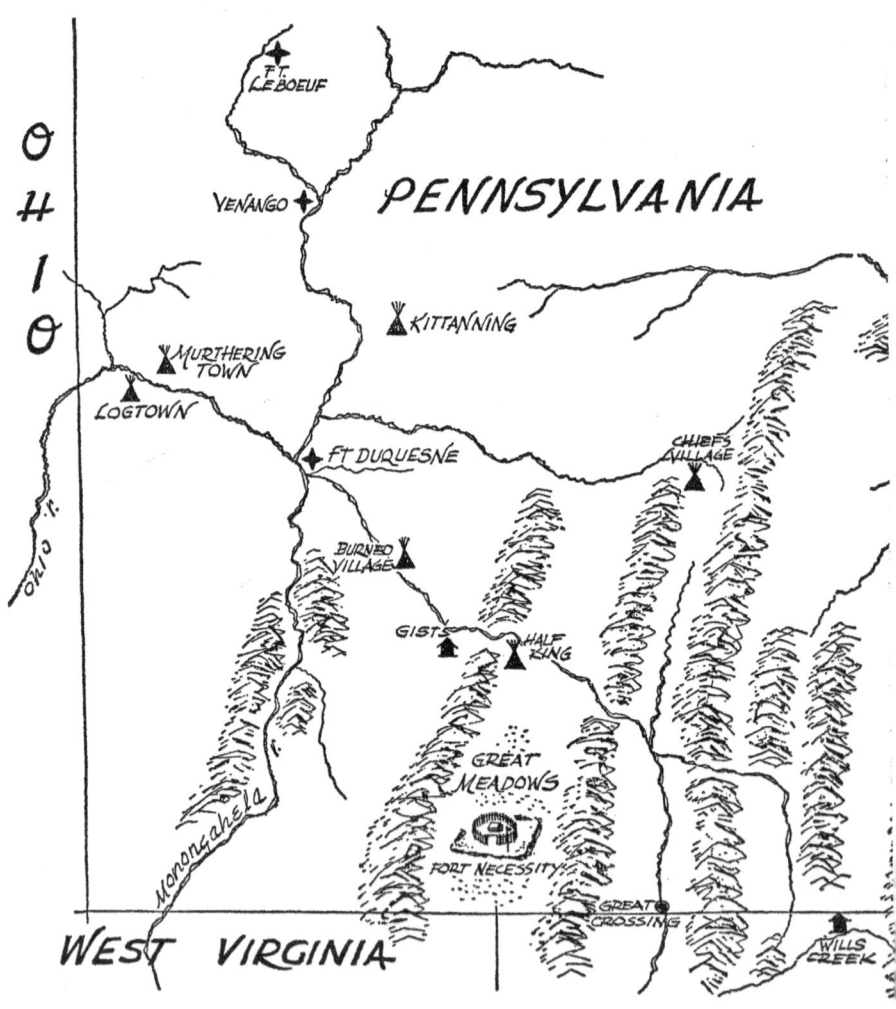

OHIO

FT. LEBOEUF

VENANGO

PENNSYLVANIA

KITTANNING

MURTHERING TOWN

LOGTOWN

FT DUQUESNE

CHIEFS VILLAGE

BURNED VILLAGE

GISTS

HALF KING

Monongahela

GREAT MEADOWS

FORT NECESSITY

GREAT CROSSING

WILLS CREEK

WEST VIRGINIA

THE DRUM!

A Novel of
Washington's
First Command

Robert Edmond Alter

WILDSIDE PRESS

To Maxine

Also by Robert Edmond Alter:

THE DARK KEEP

CONTENTS

"A land not worth fighting for
isn't worth living in."

—GEORGE ROGERS CLARK
1752–1818

1

FIRST BLOOD

Matt Burnett eased his leggings out behind him. He squirmed his chest and stomach into a comfortable position on the shocking-white snow and froze his body into a waiting statue. Only the eyes in his youthful face moved as he peered through the pine branches at the quiet, secluded Indian path. His long musket lay at his side, under the light pressure of his tanned hand.

It was late winter, the fag end of the year 1753, and the chill December sun inched slowly over the still Pennsylvania forest. Matt could feel the sharp bite of the cold snap working its way through his deerskin garments, but because of his nervousness and anticipation he could also feel icy sweat gathering on his hide.

His eyes narrowed in annoyance suddenly as he sensed the old Indian, Chief, moving in the scrub on his right.

Matt's thin lips made a tight smile. He knew what was bothering the Seneca: Chief was afraid he wouldn't get the first shot at the Abenaki that was trailing the path of the two unknown white men. And if he didn't he couldn't morally claim the scalp.

But he can have it for all of me, Matt thought with a repressed shudder. He cocked an ear, trying to pick up a movement from Shad Holly who was hidden further up the trail. There wasn't a stir of sound from that quarter. Shad had probably fallen asleep.

Matt canted his eyes downward for a moment, peering again at the strange footprints that stepped before him in the Indian path. Shad and Chief had both agreed that the prints were made by two white men shod in worn boots: a tall man with a long stride, and a squat man with a quick choppy walk.

The three hunters had come upon the trail three hours ago, at the place where Slippery Rock Creek forks, and had further found the telltale tracks of an Abenaki following the two strange white men. They had hurried south quickly, cutting away from the trail, and at the close of three hours running had knifed back into the path in the hope of intercepting the Abenaki. The double boot prints in the path now showed them that they had been successful.

But the presence of the two lone white men in the vast wilderness bothered Matt. What were they doing there? What did they want? They weren't trappers, like he and Shad, because trappers didn't wear boots. Nor, Chief had said, were they French soldiers from Venango or Fort le Boeuf, because the boots were American-made. What then?

A bird on the far side of the path began a throaty warble, then changed its mind in the middle of a trembling note and shut up. Matt's hand tightened on the musket. His thumb eased the lock back.

Thirty paces down the path a pine branch whipped silently aside and a tall Abenaki with crimson war paint on his face stepped into the trail. His obsidian eyes flashed to the snow beneath his moccasins and his narrow bullet-

12

shaped head moved from right to left as he studied the tracks.

Suddenly his head lifted high and he seemed to sniff the crisp air.

He's on to us, Matt thought urgently, but he isn't quite sure yet. He edged the musket up slowly to cover the hollow pit in the Indian's chest where it showed through his open blanket.

The Abenaki started to move, then stopped. His hooded eyes shadowed with suspicion as he stood there like a listening image in the middle of the trail. Matt's finger curled about the cold trigger.

All at once the Abenaki's head snapped to the left, his eyes blazed, and he stared at Matt's pine-needle shelter. Instantly his right hand swung up, showing a glinting tomahawk, and he took an oblique leap into a crouch, and right then Chief's musket went *KA-PLAM!* and you could see the bark and snow fly off a pine a foot above the Abenaki's hunkered head. You never could teach Chief not to jerk the trigger.

That Abenaki hadn't known about Chief, and you had to say this for him: no near miss was going to distract him from his purpose. He cocked the tomahawk over his shoulder and let out a *Eee-yu!* and came leaping for Matt, and his intentions couldn't be any clearer.

Matt swiveled his body in the snow and swung the barrel of the musket and squeezed back on the trigger. A ball of white smoke bloomed as the second shot shattered into the sullen wilderness and, blinking his eyes against the haze, he saw the tattered feather in the Indian's scalp lock sweep forward as the brave doubled into the mushy snow.

Matt reloaded, keeping one eye on the trail, as he counted up to one hundred. Nothing happened; no second Abenaki appeared. So he stood up and stepped out of his shelter.

He heard Chief give a grunt of admiration—but it was

13

only from politeness. Deep disappointment lay heavy on Chief's weather-grained face as he moved his stodgy body over to the side of the dead Abenaki.

"Fine," he muttered; but Matt thought the word lacked conviction. He knew Chief was still thinking about the scalp.

Shad Holly lumbered suddenly through the brush and stood yawning and blinking at the dead Indian. Holly was twenty-one, having three years on Matt, though his great height and rotundity gave him the appearance of being ten years older. He wiped at his beefy red face with a thick square hand, and smiled.

"I knew you was gonna get him, Matty," he confided. "I didn't have no worry about that a-tall."

"That's why you decided to take a cat nap, eh?" Matt winked at Chief.

Instantly Shad's pouchy features twisted into a lump of righteous indignation. "It ain't true that I fell asleep!" he bawled angrily. "You expect a man of my size to run through the woods for three hours like a durn fawn and then not even get to close his eyes for a minute? That's all I done —just closed 'em for a second while we was waitin' on this redstick. I didn't even doze, not even for a minute!"

But Matt was looking at the dead Abenaki again. He had no regrets over the shooting. After all, the Indian had been on the warpath. But it was the first time he had been caught up in the gut-grabbing shock of a life-and-death struggle, and now he felt awed.

Chief, however, seemed to feel nothing at all. He pushed at the dead man with the toe of his moccasin and grunted. Then he hunkered down to peer at the brave's still features.

"St. Francis Abenaki," he muttered, with a touch of disdain.

Shad pawed at his beefy face again and sniffed. "Well, that means he was workin' for the French, and it's dead cer-

14

tain he wasn't trailing no frog-eaters." He eyed the boot prints reflectively.

"They ain't redcoats, so my guess is they belong to Americans—say scouts, or maybe messengers. Now why would two Americans be coming hotfoot from Canada?"

Matt looked off at the grim wilderness, draped weirdly with sullen gray mist, all crisscrossed with the reaching black stick-arms of leafless branches, and said:

"Only sure way to find out is to catch up with them. They can't be far ahead . . . probably holed up right now wondering who fired."

"I'm sick a playing hide'n seek with a bunch of strangers," Shad grumbled. "We was gonna go home. Don't you forget that our traps and hides is clear back on the Susquehanna."

"Yes, but we think these men are Americans," Matt appealed. "And I think they're in trouble. And if they are—we can't leave 'em out here in Mingo and Delaware country alone."

Shad rolled his eyes and blew out his breath and pawed at his face. Then he threw his fat hands into the air and sighed resignedly.

"All right, Matty, all right. If you ain't gonna sleep nights without first gettin' yourself into Injun trouble—we'll go run 'em down. But I'm agin it." And, in an undertone, he added, "Hoofin' and snortin' about ever'which way . . . pure foolishness!"

The two young trappers shouldered their muskets and turned to go. Then they paused and looked back at Chief.

The old Seneca was still standing over the dead brave wistfully gazing at the prime scalp lock. Shad cocked his head slightly, watching his old friend with amused understanding.

"All right, Chief?" he asked. "Ready to get on?"

The three men came together again and moved quickly off into the white silence.

15

Moving hurriedly through the gray pall of winter, through the frost-crackling woods, across half-frozen bogs, ice- and refuse-clogged streams, up-down serrated hills, Matt, bringing up the rear, watched his two friends with a warm sense of thankfulness. He couldn't ask for better companions in the woods. He smiled, seeing old Chief's head bob down, spying out the track across a stretch of glassy marsh.

No one, not even Chief himself, seemed to know his correct age. Shad figured the old warrior was nearing seventy, but, from Chief's endless endurance and agility, Matt doubted that he was really that old. They saw very little of Chief during the spring and summer; yet each fall when Shad and Matt set out for a winter of trapping they were sure to find the old Seneca waiting for them somewhere along the banks of the Susquehanna.

Shad said that when he first went into the woods as a boy he had met Chief and had saved his life. Chief, it seemed, had lost his musket in a running battle with a bear, and when Shad came upon them Chief was trying to stand up to the bear with only his hunting knife. So Shad had dropped the bear with one shot.

Chief had made a great to-do over the incident, had exchanged blood with Shad—each pricking his index finger and placing a drop of blood on the other's tongue, making them blood brothers for life.

Matt grinned to himself, picturing a young, fat Shad and old tattered Chief standing alone in a great forest over the body of a dead bear, solemnly performing the sacred ceremony of brotherhood.

Shad was a curious enigma of frontier life; a great footloose carefree Hercules caught between armed civilization and savage wilderness. He had no idea, and not much interest, in who his parents had been. He had been brought up by a frontier trader who claimed that he had found Shad as a little child in the hands of two Senecas. No one knew

16

whether the story was true or not. Shad had always claimed that the trader merely wanted a boy bound to him to help in his business, because from the day that he was big enough to be useful the trader had worked him ruthlessly and had beaten him at the slightest sign of rebellion.

When Shad turned twelve (and already as big as a horse), he had slapped the trader over the head with one of his own skillets and had run off on his own. Since that time he had lived his life between the forests and the fringes of the frontier towns. Trapping, hunting, doing odd jobs, he had prospered in size and wit.

Wherever Matt traveled he discovered that white and red men alike knew and accepted Shad; though it was true that the Indians seemed to hold Shad in higher regard than did his own white brothers. Matt always believed that this was due to the fact that white men refused to try to understand an enigma, and not because Shad was naturally savage.

It was also true that he had heard slurring remarks made about Shad's character regarding a certain knack of his for wandering off with anything that wasn't nailed down, and a few things that were. But Matt had never found this to be true. Shad was just naturally lucky at finding odd things. Shad admitted it himself.

Now, watching Shad scramble over a litter of storm-felled timber, huffing along in Chief's nimble wake, Matt smiled and thought that regardless of what others thought of him, he would rather trust himself in the woods with Shad than any other man he knew.

Up ahead Chief had paused in the center of a small meadow bedded down in a white blanket of snow. He cocked his head quizzically, then chased himself in a tight circle, peering at the snow at every step. Finally he raised an arm and waved his two friends on.

Shad and Matt hurried up and followed the line of Chief's

17

pointed finger. A set of moccasin tracks crossed the meadow and joined the double file of boot prints.

Shad lowered his great frame on one knee and inspected the tracks carefully. "Seneca," he announced shortly. He looked at Chief.

"Friend of yours, Chief?"

Chief grunted and spoke stiffly. "Half King."

Shad spoke over his shoulder to Matt. "I know this Half King. He's chief of a small tribe near Chestnut Ridge. He's a wily old hand—got more savvy than any Injun should naturally have. He sees he's caught in a squeeze between French and English and he's tryin' to play both ends to the middle, hoping to save his land somehow. I ain't never trusted him much. Too stand-offish."

Matt saw where the Seneca's tracks had met with the two strange white men's, where the three of them had stood talking for a moment, and then where they had all continued on together.

"Well, it appears they didn't have any trouble," he said. "Maybe he's decided to throw in with the English."

Shad stood up heavily and looked off at the blank wall of white and black forest. "That's the whole trouble with that Injun . . . you just can't tell what he's decided to do. But, Matty, something's happening out here—something big. Maybe you was right. Maybe we better shag after these fellas and see what's going on."

The three friends moved on again, spearheading the lonely wilderness, jogging easier now over a wide belt of smooth rolling hills, coming ever closer to the old Indian village called Murthering Town.

Shad, glancing at the boot prints with concern, said:

"I hope them two idjuts have enough sense to steer clear of Murder Town. Them Mingoes is well named."

Matt said nothing, though he hoped so too. Vaguely he felt a strange kinship for the two men whose tracks marked

18

the face of the wilderness. He sensed that they were in danger and needed help—even though the help was nothing more than a warning.

Chief guided them skillfully around a long chain of icy ponds whose scummy fingers reached out like the spokes from the hub of a wheel, and once again Matt felt grateful that Chief and Shad were with him. He knew that a man without the knowledge of the land contours could spend a week trying to work his way out of the pond maze—going from the hub out to the tip of a finger creek, back down to the hub, or pond, again, then out to the next tip, and on and on until he either ended going in a circle or blundered onto the next pond.

Evidently the Seneca, Half King, was leading the two white men correctly.

They had entered a frozen wood and were padding along at a regulated pace, when Chief suddenly threw up his arm and stopped. Shad and Matt crowded against his back as the old Indian lifted his head and sniffed the air.

"What is it, Chief?"

"Wood smoke."

They proceeded on again, only slackening their pace for the sake of caution. All at once a sharp cry cracked at them like a pistol shot and they lurched to a halt in the snow.

"Stop right there! Who are you?"

A small, heavily bundled, booted man stepped from behind a tree and leveled a musket at them. His eyes were perfectly round and steel blue. He was bearded and, somehow, Matt thought, ferocious-looking.

"It's all right," Matt called. "We're friends—Americans."

"Who's that Mingo?" the man wanted to know. "He looks like a Laurel Ridger to me."

"Who gives a hoot what he looks like to you?" Shad shouted peevishly. " 'Course if he ain't good enough for you, why then we'll just take him away with us. I guess you don't

19

want to hear about the Abenaki that's been skulkin' your trail. No, you wouldn't care to hear nothing about that. Come on, Matt. We'll go mind our own business." And, turning, he pretended to take off in a huff.

"Hold on!" the small man cried. "There's no call to take offense. This is touchy territory. A man can't afford to take chances with Mingoes who have a yen for scalp lifting. What's that you say about an Abenaki on our trail?"

"A man can afford to take a moment to see if the other white men around him is still wearing their hair afore he starts calling every Injun he sees a scalper. Do I look scalped to you?" Shad demanded.

"Be quiet, Shad," Matt said. He walked up to the small man, ignoring the pointed musket. "We've been on your trail ever since you crossed Slippery Rock. An Abenaki was also on your trail. We jumped him a few miles back."

"Yes," Shad said, coming up to them, "but it was nothin' much. That Abenaki was only trying to run you and your friend down. He was only dolled up in his war paint and armed like a French fort. Matt here shot him dead after he'd bowled me'n Chief over like reeds in a high wind. You talk about scalpin'! That Abenaki would've had my scalp on his hip right now if it hadn't been for Matt here!" He began to pound Matt's shoulder with sledgehammer blows of admiration.

Matt dodged to one side and frowned at the big fellow.

The little man looked confused and slightly embarrassed. He tried to smile at Matt and cock a dubious eye at Shad at the same time.

"I don't want to appear ungrateful," he mumbled hesitantly. "I didn't know that—"

"Gist!" a sharp voice called from somewhere beyond them; a voice that managed the difficult feat of sounding both pleasant and commanding. "Bring the gentlemen in here. I think you've kept them out in the cold long enough."

20

2

MURDER TOWN

Two men, an Indian and a white man, were in a small secluded rock-ribbed glen. The white man sat on a log warming his hands before a fire in the snow. The Indian stood aside, slightly in the rear, and watched the newcomers without a hint of expression.

The white man stood up, moving with an abrupt gracefulness, showing Matt that he was tall, well-proportioned, and neatly clad in winter garments that strangely enough would be accepted in the best of Tidewater homes or in the heart of a howling wilderness. He was a man who would fit in, anywhere.

He was obviously a gentleman, yet not of the stiff self-important English breed. He was quite young: about Shad's age. His face was both bluff and handsome. He smiled, showing bad teeth, and said:

"Welcome, sirs! Come closer and warm yourselves. I gather from what little I chanced to overhear"—turning his warm smile on Shad—"that I owe you my thanks. I'm Major

21

George Washington of the Virginia militia. This other gentleman is Christopher Gist, my friend and guide. And this"—with an easy wave of his hand toward the silent Indian—"Half King, my friend."

Matt and Shad shook hands with Gist and the major and inclined their heads to Half King; and Chief, who liked to imitate Shad, shook hands also, but ignored Half King, who in turn ignored him, there being no love lost between a Seneca of one tribe and a Seneca of another.

The major studied Chief closely, then turned to Matt. "Is he a Laurel Ridge Seneca? Do you trust him?"

"Do you trust Half King?" Matt countered.

"I have reason to. Half King sees that the French are taking his lands from him. He has turned to me for help."

"Well, major," Shad rumbled heavily, "we got a better reason to trust Chief. Chief here don't care a hang about land, nor the French or English neither. Chief just likes me'n Matt."

Washington canted his head slightly toward Shad, saying, "That's a reason for trust that's hard to beat. So be it. Now what about this Abenaki I heard you telling Gist of?"

Matt quickly repeated his tale, thereby cutting Shad's opportunity to embellish the facts, and finished with— "Why would the French want you murdered?"

Washington was silent for a moment. He stared at the fire reflectively, then seemed to come to a carefully weighed decision.

"I see no harm in telling you that I am acting on behalf of the Ohio Company. Being trappers, you probably know that the Company has penetrated the Ohio country to the domain of the Miamis and beyond.

"But the French view this trangression with alarm, fearing they will lose their influence with the tribes of the upper Ohio Valley, and presage the ultimate destruction of their fortified line of communication between Canada and the

22

Gulf of Mexico. That is why they have erected forts at Presque Isle, at le Boeuf, and at Venango.

"Naturally the Company complained of these hostile demonstrations; their lands lay within the chartered limits of Virginia . . . so Robert Dinwiddie, one of the Company, and now Governor of Virginia, decided to send a letter of remonstrance to M. de St. Pierre, the French commander at Fort le Boeuf, asking the French, politely, to remove themselves. I was elected to carry that letter."

Shad whistled his admiration. "From Williamsburg, major? That's nearly four hundred miles!"

Washington smiled. "As the crow flies. However, to a man on horse it is perhaps double. There were eight of us in the beginning, and the journey to le Boeuf was accomplished in forty-one days. After leaving Venango on our return, we found our horses so weak that we left them and their drivers in charge of Vanbraam, a friend of mine. Gist, Half King and I have been afoot ever since."

"How did St. Pierre receive you and your demand, major?" Matt asked.

Washington appeared amused. "Much as you would expect a French officer and gentleman to do. He thanked us, entertained us for four days, and then delivered into my hands a sealed letter for Governor Dinwiddie."

Shad hunched forward on his haunches, his fat face working with curiosity. "Well, what did the letter say? Ain't you opened it yet?"

Washington looked sharply at Shad. "Opened it?" he echoed. "Why of course not. It's not mine to open. I'm only the bearer." Then his look softened, as though he understood the nature of Shad's curiosity. "I can say this much on my own observation: the French are well fortified. I'd say they planned on staying where they are."

"And how were things at Venango?" Matt asked, giving Shad a nudge to quiet him.

23

"Much the same. Joncaire is in command there. He has a friend with him, a young half-breed by the name of Cass, I think."

Matt started. "Cassanna? I know him. His mother was a St. Francis Abenaki and his father a French officer. When I was a youngster the father brought Cassanna to my father's stockade near Harrisburg and stayed with us for two weeks."

Washington nodded, staring soberly at the fire. "I couldn't bring myself to trust those two gentlemen. Oh, they were polite enough, but I discovered later that they'd gone behind my back and had tried to turn Half King against me."

"Bad," Chief announced suddenly. "Cassanna—much bad name."

Washington turned his attention to the old Indian again.

"I see your friend is somewhat civilized. What is he chief of?"

Shad beamed at Chief proudly, saying, "He ain't chief of nothin'. I just call him that 'cause it makes him happy. He don't have much to do with them Laurel Ridgers, and they don't have much truck with him. Tell you what, major, since Chief took up with me, he's decided that he'd rather be a full-blown American instead a just an old Mingo. That's why it's harder'n iron to get Chief to talk Seneca, 'less he wants to tell me something private-like.

"Trouble is, though, now that he's got himself all civilized with his English words and handshaking and hallelujah religion, his tribe sort a frowns on him—thinks he's dandified himself a mite too much. But it don't seem to bother Chief none. He didn't even kick when they chased him out a the village this summer."

"Why did they desire his departure?"

Shad looked sincerely indignant. "It's the fault of civilization, major! Poor old Chief was a victim of the white man's habits, and when he took to returning each year to his village with them habits it just got to be more than them honest

24

Injuns could bear. Seems that somewhere along the line Chief picked up the habit of walkin' off with things that was left laying around by careless owners."

He paused to glance at the sky and swipe at his mouth with the back of his hairy hand.

"I can't for the life a me figure where he picked up such a habit," he murmured in conclusion.

Matt felt that they were wandering far from the important matters at hand. He turned back to the young major. "Sir, what do you think will happen if the French decide not to pull back into Canada?"

Washington raised one eye and pursed his mouth slightly. "I personally feel that the French's attitude is the same as an open declaration of war. It may be that the King will decide to drive them out."

Shad snorted his disgust. "I've seen how that works before. The English get all pop-eyed with alarm over what the French are doing and they scream and wail like tom cats with ice water spilled on 'em— Oh, my goodness! We can't have this! We've got to get in there and whip 'em! We've got to drive them nasty Frenchies clear back to the North Pole! And then who finally goes out and does the fightin'? I'll tell you who—the Americans! That's who! Look what happened at Louisburg in 'Forty-five!"

"Shad," Matt said, "this land is as much ours as it is England's. If we help England to fight their battle, by the same token they are helping us to fight ours."

Washington nodded, his eyes curiously alight. "That's a good thing to remember," he said quietly. "England claims the land, but it is in name only. We are the land. Someday I hope that its name will also be ours."

Shad turned and peered closely at Chief. "Look at old Chief," he demanded with a grin, "laughing himself to death."

They all paused to look at the old Seneca and saw him

25

regarding them with an impassive stare. Gist stepped closer to study Chief's board-wall expression. "How can you tell?" he asked dubiously.

"You got to know him," Shad replied. Then he spoke to Chief in his own tongue. Matt, who had picked up a smattering of Seneca, could follow the flowery speech.

"What is it that delights my brother so?" Shad inquired.

"Oh my brother, is it not vastly amusing to behold the French and English and the Seneca Half King running in an endless circle, each shouting tragically: 'It is my land! It is my land!' Is it always this way with the civilized? If it be true, then I wash my hands of it. Let any man call it his land if he so wishes. Let him erect his forts and trading posts. Let him lay his boundaries and march his soldiers. I go where I please and when I please; because I know that it is all, *all* my land, and that to the children of the wilderness a name is without meaning."

Shad tossed his great head and roared with laughter. He pounded Chief on the back and winked at Washington.

"Chief's got the whole problem licked," he said. "He says it's all his land. So the rest a you fellas might as well pack up your forts and go home!"

Something landed with a flat smack against a tree just beyond Washington's head and a split second later the six men heard the hollow *plam* of a musket. Instantly they were on their feet, reaching for their weapons. Half King and Chief turned without a word or sound and blended themselves into the forest.

"Came from behind you, Gist!" Shad bellowed. "Spread out and run him down afore he can reload!"

Matt ducked into a crouch, humping over his musket, and, cutting into an oblique away from the line of fire, ran for the trees. A ragged dead thicket rose to meet him at the edge of the wood. He leaped into the air and came down in its center. He crouched there for a moment peering through

26

the network of brittle branches, opening his mouth wide so that the sound of his breathing would not obstruct his hearing. To the right of him he heard the *cush-cush-cush* of men running through the snow, and a shout or two. Then, abruptly, a Mingo darted across his path, head down, attempting to reload his musket as he ran.

Matt stood up in the thicket, covering the Indian with his gun. The Mingo came to a startled halt and stared at the young trapper with wide startled eyes.

"Hadi'nonge dedji'aon'gwa!" Matt said. We are all around you.

The Mingo hesitated only a moment, then pitched his musket into the snow. He folded his arms across his chest and assumed an unafraid attitude.

"Shad! Major! Over here! I've got him!" Matt called.

In the late shadows of afternoon the six men gathered about the strange Mingo. Shad, catching the would-be assassin by the neck in his great paw, pushed him up against a linden tree and held him there.

"Anybody know this fish-eyed scum?" he asked.

Half King stepped up and raised a finger to show that he was about to speak. "It is a French Indian from Murthering Town," he said in stiff English. Then, in Seneca, he addressed the Mingo.

The savage from Murthering Town answered glibly, his eyes leaping quickly from face to face as he spoke. Half King grunted and turned to Washington.

"He claims that he was hunting for his dinner. His gun went off by accident. He is sorry that he nearly killed my brother. I do not believe him."

"Don't believe him!" Shad bellowed. "I hope to beat myself silly, we don't believe him! He lies in his teeth, that's what he does! I'm amazed his teeth don't rot and fall right out a his head from the stinkin' lies he tries to strain through 'em!"

Gist seemed of the same opinion. He raised his musket and placed the barrel to the Mingo's head. "I see no reason why we should worry about it any further," he said fiercely.

But Washington interposed quickly. "Wait, Gist. I'm not inclined to believe our friend any more than you; but that is hardly proof that he's guilty. If war comes we may yet be able to swing his people over to our side. Killing this man will only give us new enemies."

Matt, having no desire to see a defenseless man killed in cold blood, nodded, saying, "I agree with you. But you must face the fact that Joncaire and Cassanna have set their friends on you. You and Gist are in grave danger."

"That is now quite obvious," Washington said calmly. "Gist and I will have to double our pace, as well as our caution."

Shad heaved a great sigh of reluctance and removed his hand from the Mingo's throat. "Well, if you fellas have decided to let this cross-eyed bug-eater go, we better get shed of him afore he ears in on our plans."

He grabbed the Mingo by the shoulder and propelled him bodily into the thicket. "Run you! Hy-Yi! Before I kick your breeches clear up to your ears and make you look like all legs with a pair a eyes!"

The Mingo picked his way quickly from the thicket and paused to stare blank hate at the white men. Then he turned and loped off into the mistlike gloom. Glancing at Chief, Matt realized that the old Seneca was laughing to himself. Chief loved to see other people pitched head-first into bramble bushes.

"Major," Shad said huskily, his little eyes jumping from right to left with the strain of concentration, "I guess this St. Pierre message is pretty important to you and old Dumwiddie, so here's what you do. You'n Gist hit straight southeast for the Forks of the Ohio, and me'n Matt'n Chief will angle past Murder Town and unload our guns into it as we go. That will draw them Mingoes off you, and us three will give 'em a chase clear over to the Allegheny River."

Matt caught the natural hesitation in the major's face, and he hastened to say, "Don't worry about Shad and me, sir. With Chief to guide us, we can outrun any savage born." He glanced at the frosty sky. "Besides, it's going to snow. They'll lose our tracks within an hour."

Washington smiled and put out his hand, giving Matt a warm clasp.

"You've been most helpful. Thank you," he said simply. Then he turned and shook Shad's huge hand, his eyes crinkling with humor.

"I won't thank you in the name of the Ohio Company or the King, but rather for myself."

Shad looked downright embarrassed. "That's all right, major," he murmured. "Any time, any time at all."

Washington offered his hand to Chief. "Chief of Nothing, I wish you my best."

Chief nodded eagerly. "Fine," he said, "fine. Any time 'tall!"

Shad and Matt waved a final time as Gist, the major and Half King vanished into the forest. Matt shouldered his musket with a sigh.

"He's a fine man. Wonder if we'll see him again?"

Shad shook his head. "Tain't likely. Williamsburg's a far stretch from Harrisburg. C'mon, let's stir up Murder Town."

The Mingo village nestled lonely in a shallow cup formed by three small hills. It was disorderly and laid out without meaning as many Indian towns are. A bark hut—a wickiup, Shad called it—sat in the center of the communal clearing, and around it and scattered off into the trees stood the tall conical tepees.

29

The three hunters slipped silently along the fringe of forest, skirting the eastern edge of the village. At the signal from Chief they discharged their muskets over the town, Chief letting out an ear-splitting war cry, *EEE-YUUU!* and Shad bellowing, "Hi-Yi! Try catchin' us, you eight-toed bug-eaters!"

Then they took off swiftly for the woods, knifing due east toward the Allegheny, leaving cries of rage and confusion behind, as the Mingoes came pouring out like irate bees from a kicked hive.

Shad chuckled as they ran. He looked back over his shoulder and called to Matt. "Chief's sore 'cause we didn't give him no time to put on his war paint!"

"Save your breath for running!" Matt answered. He felt confident that Chief would lead them safely through the night and away from the Mingoes, but he knew he would feel a whole lot better when they had escaped the goshawful land of bogs and thicket tangles with their unnerving aptitude for tearing at a man's clothes and eyes.

With black night came the snow, a smothering, strangling universe of snow, turning the icy forest into a whirling world of white crystals. It filled their eyes, their mouths, clogged their nostrils, froze to their muskets, slipped down their necks and up their sleeves.

Chief called a halt and turned back to inspect their vanishing trail. He grunted his satisfaction and Matt sighed with relief. The chase was over. The three hunters huddled together and Chief jabbed a finger first in Matt's chest and then in Shad's.

"You," he said to Matt. "Shad." He turned the finger to his own chest. "Chief. Fine! Say good-byes. You, Shad, go home. Plenty skins, plenty furs. Fine! Chief go now too. Good-byes!"

Shad grinned and, taking Chief by the shoulders, gave

him a playful shaking. "All right, you old bug-grubber! We'll see you next fall."

But Chief shook his head. "Sooner, sooner, Shad. Much trouble come. Spring, spring, Shad." He turned and looked off at the whorling night as if studying it for signs, or listening for words that were beyond the kin of the two white hunters.

"May. May, Shad," he said suddenly. "Maybe sooner. Good-byes!"

The two young men watched the old man hunch off into the falling screen of snow, and Matt impulsively called, "Be careful, Chief!"

And Chief's distant reply whispered back to them from beyond the ghostly shoulder of night. "Any time 'tall. Fine!"

Shad chuckled, taking Matt by the elbow. "Know what he's up to now? He's gonna cut back on our trail and see if he can't pick himself up some trophies—Murder Town trophies. That old bug-eater. He's still sore about that Abenaki scalp he had to pass up."

"Why do you call him a bug-eater?" Matt asked.

Shad's beefy face expressed surprise. "Why, 'cause he is one, that's why! I wouldn't never mention it around him 'cause I ain't gonna hurt his feelings if I can help it. But one summer I spent some time with them Laurel Ridgers and I seen 'em eatin' snails! And snails is bugs. C'mon now, Matty. If we're lucky, maybe we can get across the Allegheny River tonight."

But he stopped suddenly, grabbing Matt's arm again, cocking his head back and to one side. "Listen—"

Faintly, as though it were a phenomenon of the whirling snow, Matt heard a soft pulsating, a distant disembodied beat. It seemed to reach endlessly across the snow-clogged night to touch them with its insistent throbbing.

"Drums," he murmured. He looked up at Shad. "War drums?"

31

Shad shook his head, his fat face twisted with concern.

"No," he said softly, "not quite. But it's the closest thing. It's kind a hard to explain, it's a feeling more than a message. It's a warning drum, a trouble drum. It says: look out —men are going to die."

3

THE WARRIORS

The long, cold, monotonous weeks of January and February passed fitfully for Matt. Always there were rumors of war and threats of war and talk of punitive Indian raids along the fringe settlements and tales of the French army that was manning itself in Canada. Yet there was never anything definite, and nothing was decided. The entire country seemed to be suspended in buzzing indecision.

The snow left the ground grudgingly, and Matt spent more of his time than his father approved of standing at the stockade gate watching the turnpike that ran to Northumberland, waiting for the latest postrider.

Shad had been gone for weeks, off on one of his many mysterious errands, and he had returned only once in the beginning of February—on a horse that he said he had "found somewhere up the road."

He had remained one night with the Burnetts and was off again the following morning, saying, vaguely, that he had to "see a man about a horse" down at Wrights Ferry, "or somewhere near there." He had, he said, news of Chief, and also of the young major they had met in December near Murthering Town. Taking first things first he told Matt that Chief had been reinstated in his tribe.

"That old bug-eater!" he bellowed. "Know what he done? He was rootin' around one day near a settler's cabin and just accidental-like stumbled over an oil lantern. The lantern, you see, wasn't in the cabin when Chief bumped into it, but sort a sittin' on a stump near the chicken pen, and Chief, fearin' it might get busted out there by its lone, took it along with him. Well sir, he took it clear back to Laurel Ridge and presented it to the *ne Shadodiowe'go'wa*—medicine man, to you. Didn't them Laurel Ridgers go crazy when they seen it all lit up? Hi-yi! They almost made Chief a sachem. 'Course, ain't no way of tellin' what them Laurel Ridgers will think when that lantern runs out a oil and Chief ain't got no more to refill it with; but till it does, he's set!"

Things, he said, were happening down in Williamsburg, but just what he wasn't sure. No one was sure. St. Pierre's letter to Governor Dinwiddie had been a refusal to withdraw, and Dinwiddie had written King George, asking for orders. The King had notified Dinwiddie that he must at all costs push the French back, but had been lax in sending funds to outfit an expedition.

Dinwiddie, in desperation, had ventured to order a draft of two hundred men from the Virginia militia, and Washington was to have the command. He had also sent messengers to the Catawbas, Cherokees, Chickasaws and Iroquois, inviting them to take up the hatchet against the French. As usual, no word regarding their decision had been heard.

Next, Dinwiddie had written urgent letters to the governors of Pennsylvania, the Carolinas, Maryland and New

34

Jersey, begging for contingents of men to be at Wills Creek by March at the latest. But again no action had been taken because of the lack of funds.

"But, Shad," Matt cried, "when will they take definite action?"

Shad tossed his hands into the air helplessly, letting them fall where they would.

"Dunno, Matty. But I can tell you this, if them governors and that fat King don't shake a leg soon, you're gonna look out the gate some morning and discover them Frenchies building a fort across the road from you!" And then he was gone, leaving Matt in a grim mood of nervous anticipation.

Matt's father owned a truck house in a hamlet situated near the Harrisburg turnpike. Grouped about the trading post were a blacksmith shop, barn, and a low squat garrison house, the whole stockaded against hostile Indian tribes.

It was a rare night when the truck house was not filled to capacity with noisy travelers, settlers, militiamen, backwoodsmen and an occasional pseudocivilized Indian. And now in the last days of March, with the threat of a French and Indian war hanging ominously over the land, the house was nightly packed with rabble-rousers, pacifiers, and all kinds of table-pounders.

Everyone talked war, but few wanted to go help fight it. The travelers from other states seemed content to let Virginia and Pennsylvania handle the trouble, seeing that the trouble was in their backyards, and the Pennsylvanians seemed satisfied with letting Virginia solve the dispute; though it was said that Hamilton, their governor, had expressed his sympathy for Dinwiddie, but could do nothing with the placid Quaker noncombatants and the obstinate Dutch farmers who made up his Assembly.

Night after night Matt would listen to the shouts, arguments and table-pounding as he tended the serving counter, and he would shake his head in dismay. It was beyond his

35

comprehension how people who were actually in the same boat could sit back and be willing to let others row for them.

One night young Harry Curry, an acquaintance of Matt's, entered the truck house. Harry was a newcomer to the hamlet, having come to the Colonies only six years before. His father was a retired British officer who had left a leg behind at Culloden Moor in the famous battle of 'Forty-six, and much of Harry's mannerism came from the old school of English superiority.

Most of the youths of the hamlet would have little to do with Harry, having been snubbed too often by his haughty attitude, and Shad Holly would have nothing to do with him at all. Shad called him "a dandified nose-tilted perfume bottle with legs." But because Harry's mother, who had been a French woman, had died during the siege of Louisburg, and because Matt had also lost his own mother at an early age, Matt had always felt a sort of strange kinship for this lonely proud youth, and he went out of his way to be kind to him.

Harry picked his way carefully through the throng of noisy table-pounders, somehow giving the impression that he didn't want them to touch his clothes. His nose, Matt noticed, was pinched slightly as though he smelled something not quite to his liking.

"Evening, Harry," Matt offered with a smile.

The youth nodded his handsome head without a hint of expression, saying, "Are they still shouting war—for lack of anything better to shout about?"

"I'm afraid it's coming, Harry. The French will see to that."

"The French," Harry said confidently, "don't want war any more than we do. They merely want a share of the land."

Matt was annoyed and showed it in his quick reply. "They have all of Canada; why must they act like pigs? And be-

36

sides, how can you, the son of an English officer who has fought the French all his life, stand up for them?"

Harry's smooth thin face was reflective for a moment, then he spoke thoughtfully. "If this were to be a war between gentlemen—Englishmen and Frenchmen, I mean—I would say go to it. But it will not be. It will be fought with boors and bumpkins such as this." He waved a slim hand over the house's company.

"Backwoodsmen," he continued, "settlers, Indians, and the usual rabble. It will be disgraceful to the name of war."

Matt's temper as a rule was held in strong leash and, because he had always tried to understand the English youth, he had made a point of not taking offense at the unkind things Harry was wont to say. But he had put in a hard day and had heard enough dissension for one night, and he spoke with sudden heat.

"If war does come, you can sit at home and tell yourself that it's disgusting and disgraceful if you want to, but I'm going! And so is Shad Holly and Stefen Caspary and Tammy Ferguson. I don't know much about gentlemen and their wars; all I know is that the land belongs to the Americans and we're going to fight for it!"

Harry stared at Matt with cold eyes. "All very melodramatic," he said calmly, "but hardly probable. I greatly doubt that there will be a war. Good night."

The following morning Shad Holly returned. It was the first of April.

Matt was standing at the stockade gate waiting for a rider to bring news, when a great bellow boomed from the direction of the hamlet.

"Yo, Matty! It's come! Hi-yi! It's come at last!"

Matt turned his head and saw Shad puffing up the hill, shouting and waving at every broad step, and bringing their two friends Tammy Ferguson and Stefen Caspary along with him.

Matt knew that Shad's news must be important, for although he usually entered the town with as much gusto as possible, it being his jovial habit to shout ribald songs and to catch all the pretty girls within reach and give them great sweaty bear hugs and send them shrieking home to their mothers, on this day he had no interest in girls and songs but confined himself to mere shouting.

"All right," Matt said, as his three friends swaggered up to him, "do you want the settlement to think there's an Indian raid?"

"To hades with Indian raids!" Shad roared, as if Matt were standing twenty yards from him instead of two. "That's pokey stuff for old men and little kids that hide in stockades and throw bean bags at one or two smelly Catawbas. There's gonna be a battle, Matty, an honest to gosh battle!"

Matt reached for the gatepost for support. It had come at last!

"A battle!" he echoed. "Where?"

Shad took a swipe at his moist face and sucked in air to holler again. "At the Forks of the Ohio, that's where! Just below Murder Town. Old Dumwiddie finally got things moving; told Georgie the boy major—only he ain't a major no more, he's a lieutenant colonel now—told him to hotfoot up to the Forks and build him a fort.

"Then, when them frog-eaters come marchin' down from Canada to ask Georgie what he's about, he's gonna whap 'em over the head with his muskit and jab 'em in the pants with his bay'net and slap 'em in the face with the tips of his fingers, and say, 'This here Ohio belongs to the Americans. We don't want no frog-eaters here. Now you just count one-two-three, spin yourselves about and march out a here double quick!' That's what he's gonna do!"

"Now wait a minute, Shad," Matt said. "You're adding to the facts. Tell it to me straight. How do you know there's going to be a battle?"

38

Shad made like a windmill, waving his arms about excitedly. Then he got himself in hand and lumbered up to Matt with a dark scowl on his round moon face.

"I suppose you don't believe there's gonna be a battle? I suppose you think I made it all up, eh?"

"How can I believe you?" Matt yelled. "All I've heard so far is your wild imagination. What about the battle?"

"They's got to be a battle, Matt! Old Dumwiddie is gonna force it. He's tired a chasing himself in circles, and he's made up his mind he ain't gonna powder his wig again unless he gets Georgie and Cap'n Tram to build him a fort on the banks of the Ohio! Georgie is at Wills Creek right now waiting for reinforcements, and Tram and Ensign Ward has already gone up with a band a backwoodsmen to start the fort.

"Now, Matt, you know as well as I do that the French ain't gonna let this happen without they grumble about it just a little bit. And that's why I say there's gonna be a battle!"

"And we're going to help them fight it!" young Tammy cried, pitching his cap into the air.

Matt looked at him, then at Stefen who was grinning with delight.

"Do you mean that Pennsylvania is sending a company of soldiers?"

Shad grinned and winked. " 'Course she's sending a company," he said. "She's sending us, ain't she?" Then he broke into loud laughter and pounded his fat thigh.

Matt looked beyond Shad and saw that Harry Curry had silently joined them. Harry stared at Shad for a moment along the line of his nose and then nodded to Matt.

"Shad says there'll be a battle at the Forks of the Ohio," Matt informed him.

"Why?" Harry asked. He didn't look at Shad.

"Why?" Shad cried. "Why because Lieutenant Colonel

George Washington's gonna build a fort there! And because he's gonna ask them frog-eaters real polite-like to please go home as soon as possible."

Stefen and Tammy grinned and Shad panned his moist red face to Matt to tip him another wink.

"Very funny, I'm sure," Harry said coldly, and he turned to look at Shad. "However, it doesn't follow that there will be a battle or a war simply because the French have built three forts and the English one. Perhaps it means nothing to you that we have a peace treaty with France. Or haven't you heard of the Aix-la-Chapelle treaty?"

"The Ox-la-Chapelly!" Shad roared, and he hit his thigh a great smack. "Ain't that a dandy? He thinks the French'n Indians'n English have lived up to the treaty! Haw! Haw! Don't you know they been at each other's throats ever since that blame treaty was signed? Brother, a treaty ain't worth the paper it's printed on these days. And if you think them frog-eaters is gonna let Washington set up a fort without them tryin' to knock it down, then you just come along with me'n Matt and see!"

"Shad," Matt said, "how soon are you leaving?"

"Just as quick as you fellas get ready. Tell you one of the last things I heard; a Colonel Fry has been given full command of the expedition, pushing Washington back to second place. I want to get up to Wills Creek right fast and do some complaining. I'm gonna tell 'em that Georgie is the best durn soldier, officer, woodsman, fort-building man in the Colonies! I'm gonna tell 'em . . ."

Matt didn't wait for more. He turned and hurried to the house, as did the others for their homes, leaving Shad ranting and raving by himself at the gate.

In Matt's family, as in most families, the final decision on any important matter rested with his father. Regardless of who wanted what or how many words were said or tears shed, his father always had the last word. And this, Matt believed, was as it should be. So he sat at the board table in the gathering room with his father and the twins William and Smite, his two younger brothers, and waited with bated impatience as his father stared at the dead fireplace and puffed absently at his pipe.

Finally his father set the pipe aside and cleared his throat. Abruptly his three sons straightened themselves on the bench.

"Matt," his father spoke slowly, as though feeling for words, "I've known for years that your heart belonged to the wilderness and not here in the settlements; that's why I've never restrained you from going off with Shad. It's been good for you, made a fine strong man of you . . . but war, ah, that's another matter. You're still a child when it comes to war."

Matt said nothing. He stared at his father's pipe and waited.

"This land that the French and English would fight over is far removed from us. Why do you think it's your concern?"

"Louisburg was farther, sir, when you went against it with William Pepperell," Matt countered. "I've heard it said that that war was fought over the rights of who should have the taking of fish on the Grand Banks. You've never been a fisherman, sir, so I doubt if you went on the expedition with that worry in mind. I always believed you fought because you thought the French were infringing on the Americans."

His father was silent for a long moment, then he picked up his pipe and checked the dottle it contained in the bowl. He smiled suddenly and turned warm eyes on his son.

"I think I understand what you mean," he said simply.

In the gathering room, with the young twins underfoot, so that he tripped over them a dozen times in five minutes,

41

Matt arranged his kit, rolling most of his small needs in his blanket.

Already a large group of townspeople had gathered in the yard, and when Matt glanced through the window he saw Shad talking to his father. Then he looked again, surprised. Harry Curry, dressed in a new deerskin shirt, tight-fitting pants and polished jack boots, stood a little aside from the others. A pack and blanket roll were at his feet, a musket in his hand. He seemed to be waiting with a bored, self-contained air.

"Well," Matt murmured. "What of that now?"

He gathered up his gear and, with a final promise to young Smite that he would do his best to bring him back a St. Francis scalp, he left the house to cross the yard. Harry turned his head and nodded casually at him.

Matt smiled warmly as he approached Harry. "Why, Harry," he said, "what makes you want to go?"

"It's my country too," Harry answered shortly.

Shad was now having an argument with Tammy's father. Tammy stood back slightly with a red lowered face, and shuffled his feet in the dirt.

"But me no buts!" the old Scot cried angrily. "I don't fancy to my laddy fighting for the English! And more, I'll tell ye, I don't take lightly to his dying for them!"

"Dyin' for 'em!" Shad cried, and contrived to look aghast. "Why, Mr. Ferguson, we ain't gonna fight them Frenchies! What ever give you that idea? Say, them frog-eaters is gonna take one look at Colonel Washington's thousand or so militia and volunteers, and they're gonna roll up their eyes in dismay and cry, 'Oh, *qui-qui,* thees American fellas is some hotsy stuff! Queek, Pierre, turn you foolish self about and let us run, *may-qui!'* Naw, we ain't gonna have no fighting."

But the old man remained unconvinced. "Who might this Colonel Washington be?" he asked sourly.

"Who is he?" Shad gasped, and he slapped a palm to his forehead as though amazed at Mr. Ferguson's ignorance. "Why, he's the soldier that old Dumwiddie thinks the sun rises and sets on. Dumwiddie says give him ten officers like Washington and he'll have every frog-eatin', snail-boilin' Frenchy back whittling clay pipes in Canada within two weeks! That's who Colonel Washington is!"

"Jim," Matt's father said kindly, laying a hand on the old Scot's brittle shoulder, "it isn't a question of fighting for the English. That's something a lot of us are overlooking. These boys want to fight for us, for our land. Washington's an American like Shad; like you and Tammy are, Jim."

The old man was silent. He sniffed and stared at the ground, then looked up at the silent ring of intent faces watching him.

"Get the claymore, Tammy," he muttered.

Tammy's face brightened with a sudden spasm, and he ran to the west wall of the house, where a blanket roll and a heavy old sword leaned in its frayed scabbard. The boy fetched the sword back to his father and watched him with an expectant eye.

Mr. Ferguson stared at the sword in his hands as though recalling the glory of thousands of long-gone Scotsmen charging across a moor with nothing but blades in their hands, against the slamming English cannons. Then he gave Matt's father a surreptitious look.

"I but brought it along just in case I decided to let the laddy go," he mumbled in half-apology. "Here, Tammy, I have no musket to give ye, but this old claymore was good enough for my father, and good enough for me when it came to a hackin' ruddy battle. It will have to do ye."

Then, as the crowd cheered and as the youths were given many hearty backslaps, Shad bent over with a grunt and rooted through his pack. He came up with a silver-plated gorget, the sort of doodad that English officers wear at their

43

necks. He gave it a polish on his sleeve and placed it over his head so that it hung right over his fat throat. Then he picked up his pack and musket and grinned at Matt.

"All right, Matty?" he asked. "Ready to get on?"

Matt nodded. "Ready."

Shad in the lead, the five youths swung out through the gate and started down the pike. For a moment Matt felt rather absurd, what with all his friends cheering and waving them off.

Then, because the day was clear and bright and the fields green and rippling, and because Shad was striding along like a great war lord, muttering—Hup! Hup! Hup!—he suddenly felt that it was glorious, and he lifted his head and stared straight ahead.

It seemed that somewhere he could hear a lonesome drum calling.

4

TO THE FORKS OF
THE OHIO

There was the creek and there was the forest, both as old as time itself. Then there was the clearing and the storehouse, but they were only youngsters. The clearing had been cleared by workmen for the Ohio Company, and these men had built the storehouse for that company, and all in the name of trade. But now the scene had changed; now Wills Creek had become an animated camp for warfare.

Shad Holly led his little troop through the forest and into camp. There they paused and looked around with the bright fervent eye of youth.

Next to the storehouse was a small office building, and they were the only two constructions that looked permanent, or even habitable. There was a stretch of hutments—half-formed log cabins chinked with mud and roofed with canvas, and some of them had stubby chimneys made of

45

sticks and mud and some didn't. Then there was a collection of baggy-looking old tents. And a small artillery park; Matt counted a dozen light cannons, swivel guns mostly.

There were wagons and unmatched teams and profane-mouthed teamsters and greedy-eyed sutlers; soldiers—militia for the most part, backwoodsmen, scouts; here and there your eye would catch a bright dab of blue faced with scarlet —the blue-coated militia officers. And Indians, a spattering of them, feathered, unpainted, inscrutable spectators wondering what the enigmatical white men were up to. Men drilling, sergeants swearing, wagons rolling, riders coming, going . . .

It was a lusty place! Matt loved it. But Harry was not impressed. He grounded his musket and leaned on the barrel, staring at the camp activity with cool detachment.

"There you are," he said quietly. "Washington's warriors: illiterate backwoodsmen, as ragged as Falstaff's army. Trash."

Anger ignited in Matt's head and he opened his mouth to admonish Harry, when a blue-coated ensign stepped from the office building and gave them a shout.

"You men! Where do you belong? What company are you?"

Shad, as amiable as a big bear heading for a honeycomb, led his companions over to the ensign. "First Pennsylvania Company, major. Cap'n Holly reporting!" he informed the junior-grade officer.

"Did you say First Pennsylvania?"

Shad nodded gaily. "The last, too."

"Where's the rest of you?"

Shad looked behind and around himself and scratched his head, tilting his cocked hat all askew. "You mean there's supposed to be more?" he asked. "First I heard of it."

"Come, come, my man!" the ensign snapped impatiently. "What is your business here? What is it you want?"

46

"Want! Want! We want a help Georgie whip them bug- and frog-eaters, that's what we want! Ain't that why all these other fellas is here? Or have we come to the wrong place?" Shad looked at Matt regretfully.

"Maybe we made a mistake, Matty. Maybe we just thought this was an army camp. Maybe it's only the Ladies' Wildlife Study Group. Say, you recall them marigolds we seen back in the woods a bit? I bet these here ladies would like to know about them! I bet these here—"

"Well!" a voice modulated with amusement cut in. "I thought I recognized your tone, Master Holly. Have you come to volunteer?"

Washington, in blue and buff and a tricorn hat, stood on the porch of the office smiling down at Shad.

"Colonel, I'm mighty glad to see you!" Shad bawled. "That's what I been trying to explain to this Tidewater sol- dier: we're the First Pennsylvania Volunteers!"

Washington lowered his head, swallowing a smile. "En- sign Peyroney, I'm acquainted with two of these men. I believe we shall accept the services of the First Pennsyl- vania contingent."

"One moment," Harry said sharply. "This man, Holly, has misrepresented himself as our officer. I want it under- stood that we are not under his command. We are inde- pendent volunteers."

Washington studied the young volunteer for a stilled mo- ment, then nodded abruptly. "Understood," he said.

But Ensign Peyroney was still far from satisfied. He pointed to Tammy, saying, "Sir, that man's wearing a sword. We can't have that. A sword's an emblem of authority. Only officers can wear swords."

Tammy moved back a step, clutching the hilt of his old claymore.

"I'll not give up my father's claymore," he murmured adamantly.

47

Shad gave his cocked hat a dangerous forward shove.

"Now look here," he demanded. "If that sword was good enough to tan some English at Culloden Moor, it's good enough to tan some French in Ohio, ain't it? My goodness, what you expect that boy to fight 'em with—naughty words? daisy stems? dirt clods? That sword belonged to his daddy and—"

Washington held up his hand to stop the hurricane of words.

"One moment. I think I understand the situation."

Matt had the impression that Washington's right eye made an imperceptible wink.

"This young man either volunteers to serve us with his father's sword, or else he refuses to volunteer. Is that correct?"

Shad opened his mouth and blinked. Then he said, "That's right, colonel!"

Washington turned to the ensign. "Well, Mr. Peyroney, there you have it. We need volunteers desperately, can't afford to reject a single man; and this young man seems to have us on the spot. I suggest we accept him, sword and all."

Peyroney attempted to retain the last vestiges of his weakening authority. He pointed to Shad with a beseeching look.

"Well, but surely, colonel, that man's gorget . . ."

Washington, Matt thought, was a good politician: he knew when to strike and when to pet. He smiled genially at Shad, saying:

"Quite right, Mr. Peyroney. A gorget on an enlisted man is too much. You agree, Private Holly?"

Shad wasn't a bad politician either. He'd gained a big victory for a friend; he could now afford a minor defeat for himself. He grinned and removed the silver-plated gorget from his throat and offered it to the dour-faced Peyroney.

Washington turned away with a smile. "Let us get on to the Articles," he said.

48

Ensign Peyroney sat behind a desk, Washington standing at his elbow, while the Pennsylvania volunteers stood before the desk.

"Name?" Peyroney asked.

"Stefen Caspary," Stefen said.

Washington raised an eyebrow. "French?" he asked politely.

Stefen grinned. "Twice removed, sir. American born."

"Sign here," Peyroney instructed. "Name?"

"Tam—Thomas Ferguson." And Tammy signed the Articles.

"Harold Curry," Harry said, reaching for the pen.

Washington studied the somber youth again. "Is General Curry—"

"Yes," Harry said stiffly. "My father."

Then Matt signed and then it was Shad's turn.

"Name?"

"Shad Holly."

"Full name."

"Shad Holly."

Peyroney looked vexed. "No, no. What is the Shad derivative of? I mean, it's a nickname, isn't it?"

"Well—" Shad hedged.

"Shadrach, isn't it?" Washington prompted with a straight face.

"Well—" Shad said reluctantly, "I guess so. Yeah, that's right."

Stefen laughed and all of them grinned, except Harry who sniffed disdainfully. Even the sour Peyroney looked happy. "Shadrach," he played with the name vengefully.

"Officially," Washington said, "they'll be posted to Captain Hoag's company, Mr. Peyroney. But for the moment I want them assigned to special duty." He turned to the five volunteers.

"The ponderous wheel of army red tape has us bogged

49

down. I was promised enough wagons and teams to trans-port the army to the Forks. To date I've received only a third of what is required. However, there's no sense in wasting this waiting period in idle time." His eyes picked out Harry.

"As a soldier's son you undoubtedly realize the value in having an advanced supply depot ready and waiting for an advancing army. This position, Wills Creek, is the starting point. What we need is a halfway station." He turned to a large map tacked on the board wall.

"I am desperately short of officers. I need a capable man to lead an advance party, select a site for a supply dump, secure the supplies, and fortify the position if necessary. Can you do that?"

"Of course," Harry said promptly.

It bothered Matt that Harry never once said "sir" to Washington. There was something almost insulting about his lack of respect.

"You understand this is an impromptu action. I can't offer you a rating at this time. But perhaps later a field commission might be—"

"That isn't necessary," Harry said.

Washington nodded and told Peyroney to draw up a requisition. Then, to Harry, "Report to Captain Stephen, Curry," he ordered. "He'll arrange your supply train and assign you your men. Dismiss."

Harry didn't offer a salute. He glanced at Matt soberly and walked quickly out of the room. Washington turned to Shad.

"You're well acquainted with the wilderness between here and the Forks. I want you to select and blaze a trail for me, keeping as near to the Youghiogheny as possible. Understand that whatever course you decide upon will be used by the army. And remember that we will be transporting cannons and wagons. You may take the 'twice-removed'

50

Frenchman and the 'once-removed' Scotsman as your assistants."

Shad grunted and pawed at his face and blinked at the wall map.

"I got you, colonel. But you realize that the only known trail is that old traders' path 'tween here and the Forks, and as a military road it would make a durn fine hairpin for some lady's coff-your."

"Yes, I know. But I hope you can find me something better."

Shad's gorget was on the desk acting as a paperweight, and Shad absent-mindedly picked it up and dropped it into his capacious pocket, oddly enough, just when Washington and Peyroney happened to be studying the map on the wall behind them. Shad grinned at Matt.

"Well, Matty, it looks like the soft camp life for you. You think of me out in all that rain and muck and whatnot when you're tucked away cozy-like in one a these nice army cots!"

"Good luck, Shad," Matt said sincerely. Then he shook Tammy's and Stefen's hands, and they all smiled at each other—though Matt's smile felt a bit forced. It appeared that Shad was right: all his friends were being sent forth into the wilderness to face unknown adventure, while he was to remain in camp and cool his heels. It was a far cry from his youthful idea of stirring warfare.

The three new pathfinders saluted Washington and tramped gaily from the room. Matt watched them go with a contrite sense of jealousy. A moment later, at Washington's request, Peyroney followed them, and the young colonel sat himself behind the desk and smiled at Matt.

"Well, Burnett, did you think I'd abandoned you?"

"No sir," Matt lied politely.

Washington laughed. "Don't try to play the proper British officer; it doesn't suit you. You're too much like me—we

51

need action, movement, men on the march and hang the consequences!"

Suddenly he sat up and slapped his hands together fretfully.

"Sometimes I think this waiting game will drive me to insanity! I'm only second in command, you know. And I'm stuck here until Colonel Fry comes with the remainder of the army. Bogged here with one hundred and fifty untrained men, while swarms of French and Indians are piling up at our backs!" Then he sighed and shrugged it off.

"Well, we do what we can. I saved you till last because I want you as my courier. I need a man I can trust, a man of intelligence, and a man who knows this wilderness. You best meet the qualifications.

"You remember Half King? This morning I received one of his wampum runners, with this message: 'Come to our assistance as soon as possible or we are lost and shall never meet again. I speak it in the grief of my heart.' " Washington smiled wryly.

"What this overly dramatic message actually portends is that the French have been seen embarking on the Allegheny at Venango. So, I have two missions for you: one, find Half King and say to him, 'Your friend and brother is coming; be strong and patient.' You see, Burnett, to help Half King is to help ourselves. We're going to need him . . . need everyone we can lay our hands on, before this is over."

"Yes, sir. And the second mission?"

Washington looked at him soberly. "The second will very possibly drop you right into the lap of the French and Indians. I'm sending you to the Forks of the Ohio, to see if the rumor of the French advance is true or false."

5

"RESIST, AND YOU DIE!"

It had started to rain. The furry branches of the deep antediluvian forest dripped silver streamers of water, and Matt hunched under his damp blanket and shivered spastically. His body ached as though the weighty Shad Holly had been jumping up and down on him with both feet for ten straight hours. He wasn't used to horseback.

The bay mare under him plogged tirelessly on, blinking her big brown eyes against the light but steady fall of rain. He was on his own now; he was west of Chestnut Ridge and the Youghiogheny was somewhere to the southwest of him. He had left Half King's camp the night before.

The Seneca chief had been as strait-laced and sober-sided as ever. He had welcomed Matt without any indication of emotion, had accepted Washington's gift of a silver flask of prime brandy, and had listened immobilely to Washington's message: "Your friend and brother is coming . . ."

Then he had spoken.

"And so are the French coming. And with them come the Miamis, the Sacs, Pottawattamies, Ojibwas, Delawares, Shawanoes, Hurons, Abenakis, Nipissings, Algonquins and Ottawas. Does my friend and brother expect me to be 'strong and patient' against this savage and superior force?"

Matt couldn't pinpoint the cause of his personal feeling, but somehow this Seneca, who was famous for straddling the fence, created a sense of unrest and distrust in him. But Washington had said they needed him, so Matt did his best to placate this questionable ally.

"Your brother asks only that you will stand by him; that you will not turncoat and go to the French. If you are to be free of the French grasp, if you are to remain Washington's brother, then you and your people must be prepared to make sacrifices."

"To die is a sacrifice that has no equal," Half King told him. "Is this my brother's wish?"

"No! His wish is that you will fight for him, as he will fight for you."

Half King looked at Matt with cold, hard Indian eyes.

"When men fight with guns, men die by guns. We are saying the same thing."

But Matt disagreed. "No, we are not. A man can live crawling on his belly, which is the worse form of death. Or he can die standing on his feet, which is the only way to live. Washington does not want his brother crawling on his belly to the French, like a cur."

Half King was bemused with his thoughts. Finally he said, "Tell my brother I shall always remain his brother." Which, coming from an Indian, Matt thought glumly, might mean many things—many many things.

"I will tell him of your fidelity," he said, rising to depart.

Half King made no reply. He broodingly studied the flames of the council fire.

That was how it had been in Half King's camp the night

54

before. Matt felt it had been an unsatisfactory and incon-clusive alliance. But there was nothing more he could do about it, except hope that the Seneca's sense of honor would hold him to his pledge to remain Washington's friend.

There was a sudden shout ahead of him, then an order to remain where he was. Matt reined in sharply and peered through the falling shield of rain. He saw three or four horsemen in a small weedy clearing; then he saw more men coming on foot from the drenched woods. They had the ragged tough-look of backwoodsmen. They were armed and overloaded with heavy packs and wet and in the middle of a soggy nowhere and they weren't happy about any of it.

But there was something else wrong about them; he could detect it in their moisture-beaded, iron-eyed faces, though he couldn't guess what it was. The leader was mounted on a tall stallion and he was holding a gleaming pistol in his hand.

"Who are you?" he called.

"Matt Burnett—courier for Washington!"

"Well, by grab, it's about time! You're the first one in the two months we been sitting out in this godforsaken hole! I'm Cap'n Tram."

Matt squeezed with his knees and the mare daintily picked her way into the clearing and through the wet belly-high weeds. Tram's backwoodsmen, about ten of them, slung a tight circle around him and the captain. They peered up at Matt quizzically, all wild-haired and bushy-faced and gaunt. And again he was aware of a disturbing sense of something gone wrong.

"I was coming to find you at the Forks," he told Captain Tram. "Colonel Washington wants you to know that Colonel Fry still hasn't reached Wills Creek with the rest of the—"

"I already know that, and a good deal more!" Tram snapped.

55

He was a dark-visaged man with the quick, sharp, suspicious eyes of a man who couldn't find anybody or thing to place his complete trust in. The kind of man who suspected a blow in the back from a friend.

"You do?" Matt was startled.

"That's what I said. I know about the camp at Great Meadows too. And I ain't so dumb I don't know when I've been left out on a limb holding the bag!"

Matt stared blankly at the angrily shouting militia officer.

"I don't know what you're talking about," he said honestly.

"You don't, huh? I don't suppose you know that Washington sent a party a men to Great Meadows to build a fort without plannin' to tell me and that fancypants Ensign Ward anything about it! I don't suppose you know that Washington thought to leave the forty of us standin' out there at the Forks like a sore thumb, just waitin' for the French to come cut us down!"

"No, I don't!" Matt said. "They're not building a fort at Great Meadows. It's only a supply dump for the army—"

"Don't tell me that!" Tram nearly screamed in his rage. "I know when I'm being played a sucker! Washington never planned to hold the Forks at all! That was just a diversion to keep the French off his neck while he built this other fort . . . yeah, off his neck and on mine!"

Matt shook his head. "No. No, you're wrong. Believe me—"

"I believe what I know! Two months we been stuck out there on that point, cut off from everything and everybody. Forgotten, like as not! Then this rider comes from Great Meadows this morning and tells us they're building a fort there. Well, sonny, I can add two'n two. I know a sellout when I see it. And I told that holier-than-thou Ward, too. I told him, 'We're sold, that's what! And I'm takin' my men and clearing out, and you can go to blazes for all of me!'

And that's just what I did. We're on our way back to Wills Crick now!"

"You mean you just walked off? You left Ward and thirty men there alone?"

"Bet your left boot I did! Oh, I could a ordered him to follow, but he's one a Dinwiddie's pets and he wouldn't like to take an order like that off no milishy officer. Oh dear no! Not off backwoods trash like me. So you know what I done, eh? I gave him an order his type a God-save-the-British-Empire soldier could understand. I ordered him to stay!"

Matt thought of the valiant ensign sticking to his post with a handful of men against the might and fury of Canada, and he felt a little sick; he felt something else too—honest anger.

"I don't know where you got all this misinformation," he said to Tram, "but I can tell you you're dead wrong. Washington hasn't sold you out. He gave no orders to build a second fort anywhere. But I can see I might as well talk to the trunk of a petrified tree as to try and hammer any truth into you . . . sir!" He looked around at the ring of silent, angry men.

"Clear the way," he said. "My orders are to proceed to the Forks."

Tram sneered. "Then you'll be proceedin' by foot, my lad. We need that hoss of yorn."

Matt looked at the backwoodsmen again. There was something very dangerous about their silently staring aspect. He turned back to Tram.

"I'm riding out of here, captain. You better be dead sure one of your men kills me when they fire at my back. Because if I live to get away, I'll have you arraigned for attempted murder."

It was all he could do to keep his voice from shaking when he spoke, and there wasn't a thing he could do about his stomach; but fortunately no one could see the little cowering ball of fear he had hidden there. He met Tram's glowering eyes and raised the reins.

"Hup!" he said, and the mare started picking her way forward.

Matt brushed by Tram's off side, by the next horseman's near, without looking right or left, then the mare's muzzle pared through a small cluster of grim-looking men on foot. They stepped aside without a word. The mare headed for the wall of the woods.

It seemed a long way to go. And Matt's back felt as large as the side of a barn, with a target painted on it.

But no one fired at him. The woods closed behind him like a protective hand. It had been a very near thing, he felt, and his fool stomach felt the same way about it.

Beyond the brilliant froth of blossoms in a laurel growth the hill shelved down through the woods and seemed to hasten away toward the apex of the triangular piece of land caught between the Allegheny and Monongahela rivers. Two or three acres of land had been cleared at the very tip of the triangle and, from Matt's vantage point, the pie-wedge of land looked as though a giant had taken a bite from it.

A small thread of feeble smoke was rising listlessly into the somber gray sky. It came from the tiny clearing. Matt hupped the mare down the wooded shelf.

Coming from the woods and into the clearing that fronted the right-angled beach, Matt was appalled by the skeletal and inadequate excuse for a fortification that he found there.

How, he wondered, could forty men do so little in two months? Then he thought, Well, if the likes of Captain Tram were in charge, it's understandable.

The fort was not really a fort at all, but rather a small star redoubt, with too many of the points of the star yet to be completed. A sort of haphazard ditch straggled across the foot of the parapet, facing the union of the two rivers. As a firing trench it would make a fair to middling drainage ditch.

A peeled sapling had been set upright in the center of the muddy redoubt and a limp Union Jack hung from it without a stir of life. Matt, whenever he saw that flag, suffered the same instant reaction: he wished that they, his countrymen, might have one of their own. An American flag.

But at that it was better than the white and gold fleur-de-lis of the royal family of France. And misinformed fools such as Tram would turn this country over to the French, if the situation were left in their craven hands.

A militiaman spotted Matt and gave a shout. Immediately heads popped up along the ditch and from behind the log parapet. Matt dismounted and left the mare to browse the grass to her stomach's content. She was a good nag; she wouldn't take off on her own.

Ensign Ward was a year younger than Matt. A tall gangly youth with a sandy thatch of clubbed hair, the kind of boy who would never tan but would always suffer from sunburn. The deeply etched lines of youthful concern were as blatant in his red face as print in a newspaper.

"Do you come from Colonel Fry?" he asked eagerly.

Matt saluted smartly, then shook his head unmilitarily.

"No sir, from Colonel Washington. Fry still hasn't arrived at Wills Creek."

The news seemed to take the heart from the ensign. He looked at his handful of worry-eyed men, looked at the unfinished redoubt, at the listless Union Jack, and said, "Oh—well, then—" elliptically.

One of the militiamen jerked at Matt's sleeve.

"Listen, brother, do you have orders for us to abandon this post?"

Matt said he didn't, and that didn't seem to help the fiber

59

of the general morale. The men looked at each other and shuffled their feet, some spat at the mud disconsolately.

They were a hangdog lot, all right, and if they knew what he knew, the rumor of the French advance, they would probably go all to pieces. So Matt didn't know what to tell them. Because perhaps it was only a rumor. Perhaps the enemy wasn't actually advancing, yet. So should he take a chance on creating a panic by telling them?

"What happened here?" he asked. "I met Tram and his men this morning. Who was the rider from Great Meadows?"

Ensign Ward looked up, perturbed. "I didn't know him. He was young, very tan, and wore a beaver cap low on his head. He told us that Washington had ordered them to cross the Alleghenies and locate an advanced base of operations. Immediately that fool Tram placed his own interpretation on the news and decided that we had been left here as decoys for the French."

He hesitated, giving Matt a close look. "It—it isn't true, is it?"

"Of course not! Sir."

Ward smiled wearily. "We've been out here so long we've outgrown some of the proprieties; you might as well relinquish the 'sir.'"

"Can I speak to you alone?" Matt said. He'd reached a decision about Ward. He was a good man.

They strolled together along the beach, on the Mon side, and Matt told the young officer of the rumor concerning the French advance down the Allegheny.

It was about all Ward needed to complete his day.

"Do you think it's true?" he asked anxiously.

"I don't know," Matt said truthfully. "It seems, though, that if they were coming they'd have been here by now."

Ward nodded distractedly. He gnawed at his chapped lower lip.

60

"Well, we'll hang on a few days longer and see what turns up. No sense in abandoning the fort, such as it is, for a mere rumor. We'll have to tell the men, though. They have a right to know."

Matt said nothing. He admired Ward for his consideration, but not for his judgment, not in this instance.

That night, when the nervous little camp was bedded down between the two rolling rivers, Matt lost his bay mare. Two of the militiamen who had been assigned to sentry-go stole her and deserted.

Ensign Ward had nothing to say when he learned the news.

Neither did Matt nor any of the other remaining men.

It was the seventeenth of April.

They were awakened by a shout from the sentry on the Allegheny beach.

"They're coming! Lawd awmighty, there must be a thousand of 'em!"

Frantically they rolled from their damp blankets, springing up with their muskets, looking everywhere at once, bumbling into each other, muttering, "What? What? Where?" Panic was very near.

Ward sprang to the top log of the redoubt and balanced himself there, staring urgently up the river. "Man your positions!" he snapped.

Matt crouched behind the log parapet and peered over the rough-bark sill. A squat, chaw-masticating Virginian hunkered next to him and spat expertly into the ditch below.

"Did that fool say a thousand? Is that what he said, brother?"

Matt nodded. "That's what he said, brother."

The Virginian spat again. "Well, draggit all, I only got twenty rounds with me."

Matt had to grin. He could have hugged the man. Here was his answer to Harry's scornful "illiterate backwoodsmen . . . trash."

"That's all right," he said. "I've got ten. Maybe the rest of the fellas can make up the other nine hundred'n seventy among them."

But under his flippancy he was scared, honestly scared. They were thirty men . . . and the sentry had said a thousand! *A thousand,* for the sake of—

A whistle blew, sounding wee and flat and far off between the river and the hills. Then they saw the enemy. A swarm of bateaux and canoes came bouncing, rolling, knifing down the Allegheny. It seemed to be a vast armada of sailless crafts.

Standing like figureheads in the bows of the bateaux were white-jacketed officers. Then the rank and file, in deerskins for the most part, some in blanket coats. And Indians, their tufted scalp locks high on their shaven heads, their bright feathers bobbing, the brilliant fretwork of war paint criss-crossing their dark hawk-nosed hatchet-sharp faces.

Suddenly Matt saw the reason for the delay in the French invasion: rafts. Huge, unwieldy rafts bearing lashed cannons. He had to give them credit; it must have been a Herculean task to raft eighteen pieces of artillery down the Allegheny.

Another whistle blew, louder this time, and the lead bateau broke course and turned for the shore. It plowed its bladed bow up onto the beach and five Mingoes leaped out and grabbed the gunwales and ran the craft half-ashore. Then the next one arrived and the next and next, and now the war canoes darting in among them. Then they were working the first awkward raft ashore. They didn't appear to even notice the little unfinished star redoubt with its limp Union Jack overhead.

Ward crawled over to Matt. "I hadn't counted on cannon," he said, and his voice was as hoarse as the voice of a man on a sand-and-sawdust diet.

"Neither had I," Matt told him candidly.

"What would you do if you were in my boots?" Ward asked.

"Stall," Matt advised. "What else can you do?"

The Allegheny beach was as active now as a hive at swarming time. The French had drawn up a firing line of infantrymen; the Mingoes were already beginning to fan out and skulk along the beaches; other Frenchmen and Canadians were wrestling with the cranky cannons, doing their utmost to shift them to the solid support of honest earth.

The drums went *Dddddrum-tat-tat-tat! Dddddrumm!*

Watching the invasion, Matt realized that the first snap estimate of one thousand French and Indians had been an exaggeration of almost double the actual force.

"I'll bet there's not more than five-six hundred of 'em down there," he said to Ward, in cold comfort. The Virginian on his right answered.

"Juckies, we ain't got but half so much to worry about then!"

But the half was plenty enough. The eighteen cannons had finally been jockeyed into position along the beach and their round, black, sightless muzzles seemed to center ominously on the little matchbox of a fort. Matt watched a soldier step to the rear of one of the squatty guns and touch the fuse with a lighted punk.

All at once the cannon kicked backwards and belched a muzzleful of pure white smoke and the *KA-BLOOOM!* of the discharge rolled and caromed over the water, as something which seemed as big and iron-clad and red-hot as a kitchen stove came wailing gaudily overhead and went *scraaack!* through the trunk of a pine behind the redoubt.

The Americans turned their heads fearfully and mutely

63

watched the top of the tree break off and lean into tilt and drop point-first for the ground. Matt wet his lips.

A whistle blew and an officer in white came before the pensive guns and addressed the redoubt. But it was gobble-gobble French and the Virginians weren't at their best in that lingo. They shrugged.

"Asking us to surrender, I rather imagine," Ward suggested.

"Tell him to go—" the chaw-spitting Virginian started to say.

But just then the whistle blew again and they saw the punk come down to the butt of the second cannon and it kicked with a belch and a roar and this time the thing that came at them was like a hot plowpoint the way it tore into a section of the west star-point and sent splinters *zzzzing*-ing through the air.

Matt and the Virginians ducked into the greasy mud and looked at each other statically for a dry-mouthed moment. Then Ward said:

"It's hopeless. We'll have to talk terms. They're simply playing with us now. They could batter us to mush if they wanted to."

They could do worse than that if they wanted to, Matt realized bleakly. They could rush the redoubt in sixty seconds and bayonet and tomahawk the thirty defenders quicker than you could say Scat! Ward was right: it was hopeless. But it galled him to think he might be taken prisoner right from the first shot out of the barrel.

"I'll go with you," he told Ward.

The ensign nodded and started crawling down the line through the mud, asking for a handkerchief, anything white. Someone gave him a white shirt and he attached it to the tip of a musket and elevated it over the top of the parapet. A moment later a voice called:

"Venez tout de suite! S'il vous plaît!"

Ward and Matt climbed over the logs and broadjumped the trench together. Side by side, the flag of truce in Ward's hand, they walked over to the officer standing before the bristling row of cannon. He bowed at their approach and introduced himself as Captain Contrecoeur.

"Vous comprenez-moi? Ah, non! Pas très bon. Not good. *Vous allez tout de suite, comprenez? Allez, allez,* uh—go! *Qui!* Go! Go! *Comprenez?* Or—uh—*mort, mort!* So? *Comprenez? Mort!* Uh—die!"

Ward and Matt got it. Go at once, or they would die. Ward nodded.

"I—uh, *je comprends."*

Contrecoeur nodded happily. Then he pointed at the musket in Ward's hand. *"Les armes! Les armes! Non! Non! Non avec!"*

"I'm afraid he's telling us we cannot take our arms with us," Ward said quietly.

Matt glanced around. The Mingoes were still sulking along the beaches, heading for the woods. The French weren't going to kill them; no, they were going to turn their backs and set them loose unarmed in the forest—and let the Indians do it for them.

"No sense in arguing with a man who can't understand you," he said. "Let's clear out before those Mingoes take up position behind us."

But Ward held back a moment longer. He looked the Frenchman in the eye and said, "Thank you for nothing. You've been a perfect cad. May you die horribly of galloping lung complaint, and soon!"

Contrecoeur beamed and bowed from the waist. *"Merci bien, monsieur!"*

"You're more than welcome!" Ward assured him.

They turned and walked back to the redoubt.

"Leave your weapons and fall in," Ward ordered his men. "We're moving out of here."

65

And they did, rapidly, casting anxious looks over their shoulders as they trundled for the woods and the long shelving hill. But the threat wasn't behind them now, Matt knew; it was waiting ahead. Even so, Ward stalled at the apron of the woods to take a last look at his little fort. A company of soldiers was already busy demolishing it, using the provincial's own tools to do the job.

"It's like watching the death of an old friend," he murmured.

"Did it have a name?" Matt asked him.

Ward smiled wryly. "Yes. I suppose it was too much name for not enough fort. We called it Fort Prince George."

They entered the forest silently. The first of Washington's plans had gone awry, but Matt didn't think it would dampen the young commander's spirit. There was something indomitable about that man.

6

THE TERROR TRAIL

The retreating Virginians were moving at a good clip, though they were still doing more looking over their shoulders than scanning the hushed woods ahead. Matt didn't like it. It was still in the damp forest. Too still. There was only the labored sounds of the men's breathing and the *squish-squish* of their boots in the soggy leaves.

"Listen," he said to Ward. "I don't know much about warfare, but I understand it's played like chess. Now Indians don't know anything about chess, they only count on the obvious. So, if I was a Mingo chief, I'd deploy my braves along the ridge of that hill in the laurel scrub and then wait for you to march your men up to me."

Ward's young red face turned pale with apprehension.

"You think we're in danger, then?"

"Think, nothing! I know it. This is a Mingo ambush! If you'll take my advice you'll try to skirt their left flank, slip around 'em by the Mon beach."

It was fortunate for all of them that Ensign Ward was not a British officer. Had he held the King's commission he would have marched straight and stubbornly ahead, and then wondered why his command was massacred and himself scalped.

"Take the lead," was all he said to Matt. "This way, men."

Matt turned south and went ahead, the Virginians falling in behind him in a tight cluster like nervous sheep. Soon he heard the rush and roll of the Mon. Then, through the fretwork of the parting trees, he saw the beach and the river and, far out, a nameless island.

He didn't lead them onto the beach itself; no cover at all was simply asking for trouble. He stayed just within the confines of the wood's apron. He led them east. Somewhere ahead and off on the left the gobble-gobble of a turkey was heard.

"Like to catch that fat old biddy for supper," one of the men muttered. But Matt thought it more likely that the fat old biddy would like to catch the man. The turkey, he knew, was a Mingo.

They forded a creek; somebody said it was called Hogg Crick. And then more woods and another creek, nameless, and then they were edging up to the foot of the hill.

Again the turkey gobble sounded. A moment later it was answered from farther off. They're starting to wonder what's become of us, Matt thought. They're getting restless for their bounty of Virginian scalps. In a minute they'll start casting around.

He turned to signal the Virginians into more speed . . . and right then their luck ran out.

One of the militiamen was in the act of scrambling over a thick log litter. But the underbrush growing up through the maze of splintery trunks and branches was wringing wet and his boot skidded and his left leg shot crashing through

68

the brittle roof of the litter and he let out a cry of surprise.

Instantly a whoop sounded to the north, then another and another as the Mingo warning went down the line.

"Run for it!" Matt cried. "If you get separated, try to stay with the river! You can't get lost if you keep the river on your right!"

They took off, running like fiends possessed, unhampered by packs or tools or weapons. Behind them they heard the eerie sky-splitting *eeeee-yuyuyu-uuuu!* war cry of the Mingoes. It was a good sound, right then. It scared the holy harry right out of them. It made them run as they had never run before, because when they heard it they knew who had made it and what it meant and they could already feel the point of the scalping knife nick under their forelocks as it started to trace its quick snatching jagged pattern around their heads.

They ran!

They gathered in a sugarbush of old tall trees on the east bank of the You. It was noon and Matt said they could only wait a few minutes to see if more stragglers would show up. But ten minutes passed and none did. They counted heads.

Twenty-five men. Matt looked at Ward and shrugged.

"We didn't hear any screams, so they're probably all right. We can't wait any longer."

Ward was a good man and that was the trouble: he was too good a man to be a good officer. He worried about the individual, which is a mistake that no officer with a command should ever be guilty of. To sacrifice a few for the benefit of the majority is a sound military principle. In this case it was better to lose five than to lose twenty-five. But Ward couldn't help fretting about the five missing men.

"I think we'd better wait a little longer," he told Matt. "They might show at any minute."

"Man alive, we can't afford to wait!" Matt cried. "It's not

just the twenty-five of us here, what about Washington? Don't you see? Tram will return to Wills Creek and report that he left Fort Prince George in your hands. Washington will be concerned . . . he's heard a rumor that the French are advancing down the Allegheny . . . he might decide to move what army he has to come to your relief, not knowing that the French are already at the Forks and waiting for him to come!"

He blew out his breath and looked at the gaunt faces of the fatigued Virginians. "Can't you see how important it is that he learns this news?" he appealed to them. "Otherwise he's like a blind man hitting at a shadow in a dark room."

Yes, Ward could see all that and he was in accord with it, but he could also see that his men were dead beat, that they needed a rest before they could go on. And now that the Mingoes were off their backs, it wouldn't hurt to squander half an hour in the hope that the other five men would arrive, would it?

Matt looked at the ground. He supposed it was always this way in war—a hodgepodge of men who belonged somewhere else, doing other things, suddenly snatched up from their sedentary lives and thrown into the red chaos of sudden decision and sudden death; the good and the bad, the stupid and the wise, and the well-meaning but shortsighted, like Ward . . .

"Don't you see," he began again, quietly, patiently, "that if anything happens to us, Washington will never know that he's marching into a French trap? I don't say it will happen; I only say it might—"

He shut up between words, turning his head sharply toward the forest. What had he heard just then—the rain beginning again, pattering on the leaves? No, the rain hadn't started. It—

A bright elongated flash went *wwwhmm* past his cheek

70

and he heard the *thok* as it found the man standing directly behind him.

Someone yelled as Matt spun about. A Virginian was looking stupidly down at the foot of feathered arrow jutting from his chest. Then he started to tilt forward with a new, glassy look in his eyes. Ward caught him, held him. The Virginians turned in panic for the river, and Matt leaped after them, grabbing elbows, collars, turning them back, shouting at them.

"Into the woods! The woods, you damn fools! You can't swim that!"

Two, three, half a dozen arrows whickered in the air. Matt swung back to Ward, who was still clutching the Virginian in his arms.

"Let him go! Ward—let him go! Don't you know a dead man when you see him! You can't help him!"

Ward came out of his shocked daze and opened his arms and stepped away from the dropping body. Then he and Matt were humped over and running for a laurel tangle and it was like running through a great pane of glass with the air shimmering and trembling all around them from the heart-clutching Mingo screams.

"EEEEE-YUYUYU-UUUUU!"

Somehow Matt found himself at the head of the twenty-three men, presuming that all twenty-three were still on their feet and together. And he led them out of the sugarbush and into a leafy alleyway, calling back to them, "Stay together! Stay together!" with Ward hot on his neck shouting, "Burnett, you fool! Get 'em off this pathway! A five-year-old Catawba could follow our trail in this muck!"

"Shut up, blast you! I know what I'm doing!" He hoped.

But he honestly believed he did. He'd had a good teacher: old Chief. Chief, he thought as he ran, don't let me down, you wonderful old bug-eater!

The round shoulder of a hill appeared through the scrub

71

on his right and he turned for it, but not to seek the high ground. He circled the base. The trick in circling on your own tracks was to confuse your pursuer enough to gain time to find another, better avenue of escape. It wasn't good for anything else, because the pursuers always caught on, and quick.

But it worked the first time. They heard the yelping pell-mell rush of the Mingoes going by the other side of the sugar-loaf rise, the multitude of moccasins pounding *thup-thup-thup* on the forest floor.

Matt continued the circle, coming back on their own tracks which were now badly obliterated by the passage of the savages. He spotted a narrow deer run slicing obliquely up the face of another wooded hill, but he ignored it for the time being, even though Ward yelled and pointed it out to him again. Matt shook his head and ran on.

He started a circle around the second hill, which would finish the pattern of a giant figure 8, thinking, If I can just time it right . . . before the Mingoes catch on. Before they stop and look at each other and ask, What is this business, anyhow? Before they figure it out and split themselves into two parties and catch the defenseless Virginians in the center.

It worked. The Virginians poured into the now well-trampled pathway, the Indians still yelping and yolping around the far side of the second hill, and Matt darted under the dripping leafy overhang of the deer run and started up.

It went up for a way and then branched. Matt selected the down run. It would lead to a ravine tangled with underbrush and there would be a stream in the ravine. Had to be. And then nature decided to lean on their side.

The rains came again. Heavy, screening, eye-wiping rain.

They came plunging, sliding, cuss-muttering down the shaly bank and through the deerskin-grabbing ear-hooking eye-gouging brush, and found themselves on the glistening

72

rocks in the knee-high stream in a narrow gorge. The rushing rumbling flood-swelling water was going *pok-pok-pok* with the fat hard raindrops drumming its surface.

Matt found Ward and pointed downstream.

"We'll split here. One group is bound to get away. Good luck!"

Ward raised his hand in salutation. "I hope you make it, Burnett. You're a better soldier than I am!"

Matt grinned at him. "Go on. You'll be a general when I'm cutting roads in Ohio. Get going!"

Later Matt discovered he had only ten men following him upstream, and he wondered how many were with Ward. It would seem that the surprise attack on the You had been more costly than he'd realized.

The rain had stopped but still threatened. Fat black thunderheads leaned over the wilderness as if at any moment they would let go completely and crush everything beneath them with one grand deluge.

They had long since left the flooded gutter ravine. Now they were jogging southeast for Chestnut Ridge. It was a painful jog. Their feet were water-chafed and stone-bruised. It wasn't as hard on Matt; he was used to it. But the Virginians were town boys, not backwoodsmen, and for two months they had led a sedentary existence at the Forks of the Ohio. Their arms were muscular from the chopping and digging, sawing and lifting, but their legs and feet were out of condition. So was their wind.

More and more Matt had to pause to let them rest. When he did, they would crumple right where they stood, like rain-soaked scarecrows, to sprawl groaning and cursing on the spongelike earth. He would never call a halt until he had them inside the shelter of a sugarbush or a thicket, somewhere out of sight.

Now they were down again, like dead men, and he didn't

know how he was going to encourage them to rise to face one more body-breaking run.

The forest was still, dripping, listening, haunted. Scent was sharp and wild in the damp air. A fox targeted Matt with his nose before his shrewd little button-bright eyes spotted him. He went off in a low silver-fox streak, straight into the small doorway of a hole in the exposed roots of an oak. But it was only a trick. Matt knew that the fox knew there was a back door in the rear of the tree, and by now the little fellow was long gone into the deep timber.

I wish I had your brains, fox, he thought.

He looked at his men again, still like dead men, and shook his head. But why waste the waiting time? He'd better have a quick scout around. He walked out of the shadow pool of the sugarbush and started up the shelving face of a small humpback that screened their hidey-hole.

He gained the saddle of the rise and looked into a small clearing of sparse saplings . . . and right now his heart grabbed like an icy iron hand as he saw a party of Indians striding rapidly across the open ground. They were heading spang for him, and for the half-alive Virginians behind and below him in the sugarbush.

There simply wasn't time to get them on their feet and safely away. They were all as good as dead and scalped unless . . .

It is like this sometimes, in some people. Something ungovernable in their make-up reacts vocally and physically and instantly, before their conscious mind can sort out and select a more cautionary plan of action.

"Tohne waktan'ha!" he shouted in Seneca. Here I stand.

But only for an instant—only long enough for the shock-startled Indians to look up and spot him. Then he was off, not down the backside of the hillock, but along the spine of the ridge, thinking in his mind, in Seneca, *O'nen ni'a hau'!* Now I am going. But they could see that for themselves.

74

They let out a yowlp and one of them let off his musket, and Matt was getting out of there so fast he was quicker than Now, ducking, dodging, his legs chopping at the earth, throwing, going.

The little hill broke its back abruptly and dipped its spine down to a timber fall and sapling brake, and he went at it in a broad leap, taking off from the slope, and landed feet-first, crashing through stalky branches and whipping twigs, and then plunged ahead all grabbing hands and hacking feet.

At first he heard the *pak-pak* of muskets behind him, but they soon stopped that nonsense because they could no longer see him in the thicket. Then he heard a shout and he knew he'd been right when he'd spotted them for Senecas. But which Seneca?

"*Sgaga'di! Sgaga'di!*" The other side.

So they were going to split up and flank him, follow him to the end of the thicket if they had to. Then he remembered the fox . . . You let the pursuer see you make a dash to a hiding place; then you slip out the back door and leave him to guard the empty hole.

Matt turned back on his tracks. He started back toward the hill again. But Senecas, it seemed, also studied the habits of foxes; at least one brave (who had had the sense to remain behind and climb the hill Matt had come from) did. There he was, standing on the gorsy slope with a musket in his hands, grinning down at Matt struggling in the thicket. He started to raise the musket.

Matt snatched at a suddenly remembered word, pointing commandingly just to the left of the savage.

"*Otgon!*" he shrieked.

The Indian froze, then came to life, spinning on his heel to look fearfully around, and lost his footing on the wet-slick slope and came down in the gorse prat-first, the musket kicking *Balowm!* into the air.

75

Matt turned east and went plowing through the thicket, hoping to get out of there before the others could come legging it back to him. Otgon had been a dirty trick but a good one. He was the Disembodied One; the evil spirit who slew every Seneca in sight. Matt wouldn't be surprised if the Indian on the hill had suffered heart failure.

Now, instead of the wall-like tangle, the thicket became a thin screen through which he could see the distant woods. He was out! He stepped through the last of the saplings and started to look around.

There was a quick movement somewhere near him. He whirled, ducking, throwing up his right hand, his left pawing for the knife on his hip.

A tomahawk went *wwwhsss* over his head, thrown by the brown hand of a muscular young savage with yellow lightning flashes painted across his forehead and vermilion bull's-eyes on his cheeks.

Matt rammed his right elbow into the Seneca's Adam's apple before the savage could recover from his near miss, then sank his left fist deep into the greasy naked belly, jackknifing the man, and leaped sideways as another one bounded up from the tall grass, and tried to get at his knife again, and again no luck, because still another one pile-dived him from the rear.

They went down, the three of them, kicking and wrestling, and it was like trying to fight a man made of butter to get a hold on a grease-slick Seneca. And now he could hear more of them coming.

"He'onwe Hadi'nonge ne Seneca?" Where are the Seneca?

And someone over him shouting back, *"Ieiensdon'gwa! Sgaga'di!"* On your right! On the other side!

Then he knew it was over. They had him. He was pinned to the weed-smashed ground on his back. Four of them were holding him. He could smell the sickly sweet stench of their never-washed bodies. One of them was panting in his face,

76

fighting for his breath. His eyes sparkled at Matt and his lips jerked into a cruel grimace-grin.

Live on your belly or die on your feet . . . that's what he'd said to Half King. Well, he wasn't on his feet, but he wasn't going to crawl to death on his belly either.

"Honon'hi'dae!" he said to the leering savage above him.

Surprisingly enough two of his other captors started to chuckle. He could feel them doing it in their bellies against his body. *Uh! Uh!* Senecas loved to hear other people called funny names. It was a kick in the breechcloth to hear their brother called the Warty One.

But the Warty One didn't think it was so funny. His grimace-grin turned down at the corners and his eyes went as dark as night. He freed a hand and reached behind his back. Matt closed his eyes and waited for the first burning bite of the scalp knife.

Everything inside him turned to cold mush. It wasn't possible that this was happening to him. To Matt Burnett. And yet he knew that it was going to happen, and that when it did it would be irrevocable and it would be forever and that would be that.

He had to keep his eyes clamped shut or they would see the fear in them and they would laugh. Behind his eyelids he saw a flicker of shadow pass across the red-brown blur that was the sun. He sucked in his breath.

"Then'en," a voice spoke over him. No.

Matt opened his eyes, blinked against the sun, and looked again at the Seneca who was standing in his blanket above him.

It was Chief.

7

THE LAMP BURNS LOW

So he had fallen into the hands of the Laurel Ridge Senecas!

At first his heart leaped with relief at the sight of good old Chief; but then his inner instinct spilled cold water over his blaze of joy. After all, what could Chief do if his brother braves wanted to kill Matt? He wasn't really a chief, a sachem, at all; he was just another warrior.

He was an elder, to be sure, but that didn't chop any wood when the young braves were on the warpath. But wait ... hadn't Shad said that Chief had become a big man in his tribe, after he'd presented the *ne Shadodiowe'go'wa* a burning lantern? Maybe there was still hope. At least they hadn't killed him, yet. They'd stopped when Chief said no.

Chief looked at him without a wink of recognition, and Matt caught the hint. He stared back blankly. The Seneca were beginning to argue.

The brave who had been called the Warty One was for killing Matt out of hand, here and now. Chief was against

78

it. His point of view was that Matt would make a fine hostage, should they ever need one.

"Oh my brothers, listen to me!" he said, with oratorical dramatics.

There were twenty-some of them, and they gathered around him agreeably, to squat on the ground and listen. They dearly loved a powwow.

"First come the French, then the English. This is my land! says one. No, mine! says the other; and who listens to the Seneca whose land it really is? None! Take up the hatchet, say the French to the Seneca, fight for us! Take up the hatchet, say the English, fight for us! And when the fighting is over, when the Seneca braves lie rotting in the woods and the Seneca squaws sit wailing in the burned villages, who is left to claim the land? Only the French or the English, for they are many! But the Seneca, no! For they are few."

"Na'e! Na'e!" some of the braves chanted. It is even so!

"Now they have come to our land again," Chief pressed on. "Now for many moons you have heard the warning of the drums and know that many men will die. And how will you answer this time when you are asked to take up the hatchet once more? To which side will you offer your scalping knives? *Da! Onen!* So now I will tell you what *ne sga't Hawennio,* the Great Spirit of all wisdom, would do. He would pause, he would listen, he would look, he would think! He would decide beforehand which side will be the victor, and to that side he would offer his knife!"

There was no end of enthusiastic *Na'es* for Chief's lengthy double talk, which, when you came right down to it, said very little.

"Then'en!" cried the Warty One. "No. This is no brave who speaks," pointing defiantly at Chief. "This is *ne Eia'dagen'tci,* the Ancient Grandmother! The old woman! Do not listen to her. I say the French will win! I say we must go to

79

the Forks of the Ohio and help them destroy the English! I say we shall be rich in scalps!"

"And I say the English will win!" Chief said.

Then they all got into it and they created a vocal bedlam. The one result important to Matt was that they seemed to forget all about him, whether they should kill him or not. The big question was should they fight for the French or the English?

In the end, as the weary sun was crawling down the sky toward its western bedroom, nothing had been decided, except that the war party would continue on its way to *ne Hanisheonon'ge's* lake, the Evil Lake, and there wait for a rendezvous that had evidently been arranged previously. With whom, Matt had no idea.

They lashed his hands behind his back, put a cord around his neck and led him like a dog on a leash, traveling at their customary jog trot. It was tricky work for Matt, keeping up, but he did it—had to; the Warty One was just looking for an excuse to knife him.

The cliff stood up from the piny woods. Straight up from the scrubby second growth and the sassafras and chicken oak and the ferny tangles of young locust, until it cut a flat rock barrier across the gray-wash sky. It was solid rock, like mountain rock, and its face was perpendicular like the wall of an old tall castle. It was five hundred feet high.

At one place there was a two-hundred-yard setback in the cliff, as though the finger of God had dug out a bay formation in the shape of a half bowl. It was this bowl that held the little clearwater lake, the Evil Lake. The place had a bad name, very bad.

The war party made camp on the shore facing the half bowl, the indented cliff looming above them like a primordial battlement. They made a fire and settled around it on their backsides to toast their wet shriveled feet. Then they

80

doctored their feet with bear grease and worked the grease into their moccasins too.

Two of them dug into a sumac growth and uncovered an old bark canoe. It was a dangerous-looking craft; Matt didn't know that he'd care to trust it on water. But the Senecas only wanted it to fish from. They carried it to the shore and shipped it. Matt noticed that they only went a little way out.

It was understandable. *Ne Hanisheonon'ge* lived at the back end of the little lake, up in the cliff, so they believed.

Chief wandered over to Matt with a chunk of bear fat for his feet. He untied Matt's wrists and offered him the fat. The Warty One looked up from across the fire angrily.

"*Then'en!* He will escape from you, old woman!"

"*Ha-ha!*" Chief gave the Seneca cry of contempt. "*De'-osthon!*" Not a chance. "My knife is as quick as the tongue of *ne ge'gach'ys*, the lizard." He turned to Matt and winked covertly.

"How that Shad?" he whispered in English.

"Good. He's with Washington. They seek a road to bring the English army to the Forks. Chief, will the Seneca fight for the French?"

Chief pursed his flabby lips and looked unhappy. "Trouble, Matt. Much trouble. Many moons runners come Laurel Ridge ask our *ha' sennowa'nen*, our chief, fight for northern brothers." Then he broke into Seneca softly. "*Da! Onen!* It is easy for them—the Abenakis, the Ottawas, the Pics and the others. They live in the north! They come with the French to protect them. They make war away from their hunting grounds. Then they leave. But what of the Laurel Ridge Seneca? They must continue to live here—on the fringe of the Dawn Land men, the English." He shook his head. It was a great problem.

"Our *ha'sennowa'nen* listens to the wampum runners, he

81

sways like a thin reed in a meadow wind, this way, that way. Our young braves think only of the moment and of the scalps. They vote war! *Ha'sennowa'nen* smokes his stone pipe, he asks it many questions. But there is no answer."

"Then why is the war party here on the Youghiogheny?"

"Continue to listen. We are here for a rendezvous with the French. The French fear to send a small party as far as Laurel Ridge, so we have agreed to meet them at the Evil Lake. If they can sway our judgment, we will continue on to the Forks and fight for them. *Na'e.*"

Matt frowned apprehensively. He knew that Chief was actually telling him that most of the Seneca braves had already secretly made up their minds to fight for the French.

"Can't you stop them, Chief? Can't you sway them? Aren't you an important man in your tribe, now?"

Chief looked more unhappy than ever.

"*Na'e,* it was so, but no longer. The English lamp I brought to *ne Shadodiowe'go'wa* burns low. It was almost dead when we left Laurel Ridge. That is why I am here. It would be foolish for me to be there when it dies."

The wily old fox had a point, Matt could see.

"Listen, Chief, what are my chances here?"

"Bad, Matt. Much bad," Chief told him frankly. "Only a bird could escape the Seneca in these woods." He cast a quick glance over his blanketed shoulder at his brothers. "But *non—*"

It didn't mean no as the French used it; it meant perhaps—

Matt leaned forward eagerly as Chief turned back to him.

"Does my brother have the courage of *ne Gaha'ciendie'-tha,* the fire dragon?" Chief wondered.

It seemed to be asking quite a bit, but Matt nodded shortly. He was willing to try anything. Chief's voice dropped even lower.

"Then here is what my brother must do . . ."

It was late in the moony night when the French party arrived. There were two Frenchmen, a St. Francis Abenaki, and another man. It was this fourth man who caught Matt's attention; there was something familiar about him. He was as dark as an Indian but his eyes in the firelight were glassy blue. He wore a deerskin jacket, tight pants and jack boots. His head was shaven and a feather was in his scalp lock. He might have been nineteen, twenty.

The Frenchmen were not at all concerned with Matt. They spoke Seneca like Senecas and they wasted no time in commencing to harangue the war party. But the enigmatic young man in the jack boots came closer to inspect Matt. Then Matt saw that he was a half-breed.

"Don't I know you?" he asked in English.

Matt nodded. "You're Cassanna, from Venango. You taught me how to throw the tomahawk, when we were young."

Cassanna's dark features were very straight, almost handsome. He smiled somewhat and hunkered before Matt.

"That's right. You're Matt Burnett, from the Susquehanna. How did you come to this sorry state?" indicating Matt's lashed wrists.

"I was with the Virginians who tried to hold the Forks against Contrecoeur. The Mingoes chased us. Later I was caught by these Seneca."

"It is regrettable," Cassanna said, without emotion. "Tell me, Burnett, how many men does Washington have under him?"

"I don't know."

"Has he left Wills Creek yet?"

"Where's Wills Creek?"

Cassanna's eyes became obsidian. "There are ways," he said slowly, "to make you more cooperative. These Seneca

83

dogs would, I'm sure, welcome a chance to explore those ways."

"That's right," Matt said shortly. "So I might as well tell you. He has two thousand men and he marched from Wills Creek a fortnight ago. He should be here any moment."

"You're lying!"

"That's right. And if you torture me I'll tell you more lies, and still more, and in the end you won't know what to believe."

Cassanna studied him for a long cold moment. Then he seemed to relax. He smiled again, thinly. "You always were as tough as whang leather, even as a boy. I should have remembered that."

"And you should also remember that my father treated you and your father as friends, when you were a boy."

Cassanna nodded. "I do remember." Then he looked away, at nothing, his eyes reflective with inner thoughts. "It's a pity it must come to this between you and me. But there is no hope for it. The English must be driven back to the coast. Even farther!"

"Why?"

"Because this is our land! The Indian's!"

"Then what do the French want with it?"

Cassanna's eyes blazed. "My father's people will drive the English from the land of my mother's people!"

"Yes, and take it for themselves. And leave your mother's people in the cold." Suddenly Matt sensed something tragically pathetic about this strange man of mixed blood and mixed emotions. The world had passed him by. This vast brawling rugged raw new land had gone beyond him, beyond all the redmen, and it would never again turn back for them. There was no catching up.

The lamp, it seemed, was also burning low for an entire race.

Abruptly Cassanna stood up. He was angry but his anger

84

wasn't against Matt, but rather against the inevitable future which Matt recognized and which he, Cassanna, sensed.

"Not while I breathe!" he vowed hoarsely.

"Good luck, Cass," Matt said gently. He didn't know what else to say.

The powwow dragged on like a lame turtle. Everyone had to have his say and everyone's say was a very long one. Once the Warty One even hauled in the ancient Seneca version of Genesis:

"Ne gwa, gi'on, hadi'nonge ne hen-non'gwe!" In the beginning, so it is said . . . And that took an hour in itself.

Suddenly Matt was aware of a slight movement in the damp leaves just behind the tree his back was propped against. He looked at the circle of savages and Frenchmen, but he couldn't spot Chief.

He sucked in his breath and looked to his right. A Seneca with a musket squatted four paces away listening to the powwow. He was supposed to be Matt's guard. Matt leaned forward a little, bringing his lashed arms away from the trunk of the tree.

The guard glanced at him and Matt yawned and shook his head sleepily. The Seneca turned his attention back to the powwow. Something ice cold touched Matt's left wrist. That was Chief's knife. The old boy had slipped away from the council fire and circled around behind Matt in the dark, just as he'd promised to do.

Now Matt could feel the blade chewing at the lashings on his wrists. He gave a tentative tug and felt that his arms were free. He let out his breath, studied the situation before him.

Chief had told him what he must do, and the time to do it was now. The guard was still attuned to the powwow and the powwow was as vociferous as ever. The moon was waning.

All right, he thought, why are you stalling? *Do it!*

He cast a handful of dirt into the guard's eyes, at the same

85

time levering his body up from the ground and, with the guard's startled *Yi!* ringing in his ears, he bolted across the clearing, dodging to the left of the surprised powwowing savages, ducking under the grabbing embrace of a Seneca who whirled too late, side-stepped another and straight-armed him into the fire, and took off down the shadowy beach for the old bark canoe.

A gun went *Plam!* like a board slapping the side of a barn, and was instantly answered by a shrieking Seneca. *"Then'en!* Would you shoot us as well, brother?" So they couldn't shoot at him for fear of hitting each other in the dark. Good!

He shot off the steeply pitched bank and into the water to his thighs, grabbed the gunwale of the canoe and started to lunge it into the shallows.

There was a swish of branches in the locust just above him and he looked up to see a leaping savage looming against the pale moon like a silhouette cut from tin.

Matt switched the canoe at a sharp right angle and the Indian came down where the bow of the canoe had been a split-second before and his legs folded under him as he hit the bottom and his body and head jacked out of sight with a crash of black water.

Matt shoved off, kicking with his feet and throwing his body half into the precariously wobbling canoe. Madly he groped around in the black trough of the craft for a paddle, found one, came to his knees and started digging at the water overside.

Bright stabs of orange flame sparked along the dark bank, and the musket balls went *spuk-spuk* in the water around the canoe. His arms rose, reached, dug in, hauled back, rose, reached . . . the dripping paddle winked silver in the moon-light.

He didn't let up his rhythm until he was halfway into the small lake. Then he rested the paddle across his knees and

looked back. He could see the black hem of the forest clos-
ing off the mouth of the bowl-shaped bay, and the merry
glow of the fire, and men flicker-legging in front of the
flames. He felt quite certain that the Seneca could still see
him. He was only a hundred yards out and the moon was
bright on the lake.

But they didn't fire at him. They didn't have to. They knew
he was in a cul-de-sac, a blind alley. Sooner or later he
would have to come back. There was nothing at the other
end of the lake—except the tall cliff and *ne Hanisheonon'ge,*
the evil He-Who-Dwells-in-the-Cave.

8

STAIRWAY
TO THE EVIL ONE

The legend was as old as the oldest living Seneca's grandfather's grandfather's grandfather. And maybe older . . . Indians do not concern themselves with dates and calendars.

It is said that once long ago *ne Hanisheonon'ge* came from his caves in the Alleghenies and laid waste to the land with his evil powers. The Seneca retreated from his wrath. They fled to the Youghiogheny and to the little nameless lake nestled in the mighty cliff and there, cornered, trapped, they awaited in fear for the coming of the Evil One.

But the *ne Shadodiowe'go'wa* was a shrewd man and, in his desperation to save his people, he concocted a scheme. Soon, horrors undescribable, *ne Hanisheonon'ge* came raging down to the little lake and prepared to smite the Seneca low with one blow. Then the medicine man spoke:

"You may kill us, but we will return. For you cannot kill

ne Eia'dagen'tci, the grandmother of the earth!" And he pointed across the lake to the far indented wall of the cliff. "Behold! She lives in a cave high in the cliff, and there is no way you may reach her to destroy her!"

Ne Hanisheonon'ge couldn't believe there was no way he could reach *ne Eia'dagen'tci.* It threw him into a terrible temper. It also threw him into the medicine man's trap. He ordered the Seneca to carry him to the far base of the cliff in their canoes. He ordered them to build him a ladder up the face of the cliff so that he might climb up and smite *ne Eia'dagen'tci* good and proper. And these things the Seneca did.

And *ne Hanisheonon'ge* climbed the ladder to the cave. And there was nothing there but some old bones eagles had left. And the Seneca quickly paddled their canoes back to the shore and left *ne Hanisheonon'ge* stranded in the cave in the cliff. And there he had been ever since.

That was the way the Senecas accounted for the stairway in the cliff. And, Matt thought, it was probably as good a way as any other. Actually no one knew how, when, or why the stairway had been built. Undoubtedly it was the work of some dim long-gone Indian tribe. And, undoubtedly, it was very old; probably older than the Pilgrim Fathers, from the condition of the wood.

Matt drifted to the base of the looming cliff and looked up. God might have used a plumb line in forming the face of the cliff. It was that sheer.

Six-foot poles had been driven into the rock wall of the cliff, unsupported at the outer ends like a ladder with one of the side frames missing. There was an open space between each wooden rung of one yard. The giant toothpicks were set in the wall on an inclined plane, so that a climber did not scale the ladder straight up but always on an angle.

It was no place for a person with a fear of heights; in fact, it was psychologically bad for anyone. Because of the lean-

89

ing separation between each of the great rungs, a climber was always faced with a fat void grinning at him. It wasn't *ne Hanisheonon'ge* a man had to fear, Matt thought, so much as vertigo.

He wondered how many of these wooden teeth there were between the water and the cave at the top. He couldn't tell from his position at the foot of the cliff, and it wouldn't do any good worrying about it. The thing had to be done. It was his only way out.

Cautiously, he stood up in the wobbly canoe and reached for the bottom rung jutting over his head. The pole was a good eight inches in diameter and it felt substantially embedded in the wall.

He sucked in his breath and lunged upward, throwing his right arm completely around the thick rung, pawed for leverage with his feet on the rock and scrambled up to the questionable security of the first step.

He was standing on the bottom rung, his left hand resting on the second rung, his right arm over his head grasping the third rung with his hand. That's how he would have to go it: pull up with right hand, raise left foot to second rung, lift left hand to fourth rung, right foot to second rung, and so on.

He looked at the space between the second and third rungs. The surface of the water waited for him ten or eleven feet below. Already it looked like a mean drop, and he had only taken the first step!

He started up; right hand, left foot, left hand, right foot. The leaning space between the giant toothpicks grew deeper and deeper. Ninth . . . tenth . . . eleventh . . . he counted them as he climbed.

Fourteen . . . lean forward, catch the one above fifteen, look at it, test it, all right, solid enough . . . raise up . . . fifteen . . . lean forward . . .

Yes, the stairway was very old. And being exposed to

90

decades of weather hadn't helped much. Neither had the wood-boring insects. The twenty-first pole felt strange to his left hand, something wrong with the tactile texture of the wood. His fingers dug in and came away with a rotting handful of chunky splinters. Dry rot.

He moved his hand closer to the wall and tried the pole again. Seemed solid enough there . . . He went up, hugging the wall around the weak place. The space between the rungs leered at him emptily.

There was a change in the sky. A pink hue was creeping across the face of the cliff. When he paused and looked out he could see across the lake and far over the roof of the distant forest, to the slender golden thread of the Youghiogheny.

The sun was climbing merrily. Matt wished that he could too.

Way down on the thin strip of shore he could see the little antlike figures of the Seneca. They were watching him. And he thought, They can see me. They can hit me from there with their guns.

Then he thought, No, they won't. They're waiting to see what good old *ne Hanisheonon'ge* will do to me.

The trouble with daylight, he realized, at the thirty-third pole, was that you could see all the way down to the lake far far below. He hated the blasted empty space between the rungs! He concentrated on not looking down. He kept his eyes on the tread rungs stepping on up above him.

He couldn't believe what he saw as his right hand clutched the fifty-first pole. There was no fifty-second pole. The tooth was missing.

He hesitated, telling himself, All right, it was bound to happen sooner or later. It only makes six and a half feet between fifty-one and fifty-three. You can do that.

But he didn't like it just the same, not at all.

Gingerly, he drew himself up on the fifty-first rung, lean-

91

ing his trembling body against the rock wall, and then straightened up slowly, reaching up and out for the fifty-third. And grabbed it.

He set his right foot on the short snaggle stump of the missing rung, and then stepped upward, lunging, throwing his right arm over and around the fifty-third pole, then, his legs swinging free in the air, jacked his body up and got a clutch on the next pole above.

Fifty-five . . . sixty . . . seventy . . .

His arms were keen knife blades of pain. His lungs hammered on the door of his chest for air. His legs were like two aching lead pipes. And worse, whenever he'd forget and glance down, vertigo would instantly swim through his head. Dizzy dizzy dizzy.

He closed his eyes and rested, standing on eighty-five, his back to the cliff, hip against eighty-six. The sun was warm, friendly, there on the wall. He was very tired. He . . .

He started and clawed at a rung for support. It was a hades poor place to fall asleep. Down was far down. He rubbed his face energetically, and looked up. Where was the top, for golly sake?

He started climbing, mechanically. Off to find it.

One hundred and seven was missing.

He went through the same gymnastics he'd executed in the fifties to get around it. One-ten . . . one-twenty . . . one-thirty . . . lean forward, grasp, lift, drag upward, lean forward . . . The sweat ran from his body in rivulets, into his eyes now. He pawed at it, cursed it. He climbed.

When he saw the toothless gap between one hundred fifty and one hundred fifty-three he wanted to scream. For a vivid moment he didn't know what else he could do.

Two rungs in a row were missing!

He held on to himself, somehow. He breathed deeply and he contemplated the grim situation. The face of the sheer old cliff might look as slick as a pane of glass from a distance, but when you were against it you could see the pocks and tiny fissures which were like a network of fine wrinkles on the old old rock skin.

One hundred fifty-three was better than ten feet above him. The vacant space in between yawned hungrily. He didn't dare look down. He slipped off his moccasins, shoved them inside his deerskin shirt, placed his left foot on the splintered stump of one fifty-one and raised himself slowly, his body flat against the wall.

His sore fingers went crawling exploringly across the rock, seeking pits, cracks, holds. He found some, threaded his right foot between his left leg and the wall and set his toes on a two-inch ledge, and stepped up on that, crane-like, his left leg now swinging on ahead for another bit of ledge, and then his left hand crawling across the wall again hunting for another fissure.

Now he had reached the jagged tusk end of one fifty-two and, with careful manipulation, set his right foot on it. He was going to have to risk a leap. Playing the human fly was already too much on his bleeding numb fingers and lead-weight arms.

He stalled, clinging, getting his breath, then sucked it in and took a quick shoving step upwards, and for a wild moment he seemed to be standing on air as all of that great brawling rugged savagely fresh land spread before him, reaching for him, down-dragging at his equilibrium, and then he was wrapping himself around the wooden rung and loving its tactile solidness with all his heart.

He swung himself up and looked down and laughed. He couldn't help it—he felt a little crazy.

He could see the end now, could count the rungs between himself and the lip of the cave: one ninety-six . . . ninety-seven . . . ninety-eight . . . it was going to come out on two hundred exactly.

Wearily, grimy, gasping, he hauled himself over the edge

and collapsed on the little shelf protruding from the mouth of the cave. He was lying on *ne Hanisheonon'ge's* doorstep.

Then he heard something shocking. It came from far far below.

Yipping.

He turned and looked down at the sliver of beach. The Seneca were cheering him! You just never could tell about an Indian.

There wasn't much to *ne Hanisheonon'ge's* cave. It was just a niche in the wall. The tiny bones and skulls of field mice and other rodents were scattered on the rocky floor amidst a helter-skelter of feathers.

There were other bones, too, of a man, a very long powerful man. Stone jars were by his side and curious archaic weapons made of flint and stone. There were writings engraved on the wall, but they meant nothing to Matt.

He looked at the old long-dead, long-forgotten warrior out of another Indian age, and felt a sense of wistful sorrow. *Ne gwa, gi'on . . .* in the beginning . . .

"Rest in peace *ha'sennowa'nen*, Chief," he murmured.

Thanks to the nature of erosion the fissures from the brow of the cliff down to the cave twenty feet below were as broad and deep as a log cabin's chimney. Matt scaled them without mishap.

As he gained the top he heard a long-drawn wail from below, and he grinned fleetingly. The Seneca were expressing their wonder at *ne Hanisheonon'ge's* mercy. It was stupefying to them that the Evil One would allow Matt to enter and leave his home with impunity.

Matt raised his hand and tossed them a wave. Then he turned and ran for the down-shelving woods, taking pains that he didn't leave glaring tracks behind him.

You just never could tell about an Indian.

9

GREAT MEADOWS

He had been on the run for days; so many in fact that he had lost track of them. It had been because of the detour.

A band of horned Ottawas had jumped him on the nineteenth. He had been forced to run north and he had to go almost as far as the Delaware town of Kittanning before he could shake them. They had used the ring hunt on him, spreading themselves into a two-mile-wide circle around the place where they had last seen him.

Every time they flushed him they would chase him until he was able to dodge them again. Then they would form another circle from that point. He didn't know how many rings he had escaped through.

Finally, striking eastward, he had lost them for good; then he'd doubled back to the south, striking for the valley between Laurel Ridge and the Alleghenies.

He passed by Chief's village one morning at dawn, and the Indian dogs had come out to yap at him. But that had been all right; Matt knew that all the braves were up on the Youghiogheny. No one had bothered him. It was late the following day when he found Nemacolin's Path and turned southeast for Wills Creek.

The primordial forest was as dense as a wall. He almost walked into Washington's advance guard without seeing them; that is, they almost killed him before he could see them.

He heard the whomp of a ball strike an elm he was passing and then heard the flat *pak!* of the musket as he dove for the ground. Belly-flat he started worming for a sumac bush.

"I got one!" a high-pitched frantic voice shrieked. "They're right smack ahead of us! I just hit one!"

Only then Matt realized he was being fired on by Virginians.

"Hold your fire, you cross-eyed fool!" he shouted in a passion. "I'm Matt Burnett! An American!"

He heard one man call to another: "Says he's Matt Burnett! Who in hades is Matt Burnett?" And the reply: "I dunno an' I ain't carin'. Put another shot in him. Thought you said you hit him!"

"Washington's courier!" Matt yelled. "Hold your fire. I'm coming in!" He stood up and wagged his empty hands in the air and started walking down the overgrown path. What in tarnation was wrong with those fools anyhow?

"Brother, if you got any tricks up your sleeve," an unseen man called, "I'm gonna put a bullet up your navel!"

"You'll need better aim than your friend, then. Otherwise me'n my navel could tramp all the way to Alexandria and still be in one piece!" Matt was fighting mad.

Suddenly a man rose from the scrub and pointed a musket at him. He looked downright scared. Then another man stood up and another one.

"All right," Matt said, showing his empty hands again.

96

"I'm not going to hurt you. I don't have any rocks to throw."

They gathered around him slowly, eying his tattered deerskins and ribboned moccasins curiously. "Where you from, brother?"

"From the Forks. I've been dodging Indians for a week or so. Are you Washington's advance guard?"

"Yeah . . . say, what's it like up ahead? How'd you get around that great dismal swamp with all the quicksand 'n sinkholes 'n gators?"

Matt looked at the man blankly. "The what?"

"What about that mountain barrier with the boulder avalanches ever' hour?" the second man inquired eagerly.

Matt gawked at him. "Avalanches? Gators . . ."

The third man had him by the elbow, shaking him urgently. "Listen, brother, is it true we got to cross a river a mile wide agin tidal waves ten foot high?"

Matt started to laugh. "Oh, sure, sure. And there's a forest up ahead where the trees don't have any tops and they grow from the ground on a slant and hold you back like an abatis of spears."

The advance guard didn't think it was funny. They looked at him with suspicious apprehension. Then he realized they were serious!

"Good Lord, you don't mean you actually believe all that nonsense, do you? Who's been telling you these lies?"

They didn't say. They wouldn't look at him either. They shuffled their feet in embarrassed anger and glanced at each other covertly.

"Listen," Matt implored them, "it's nothing but a pack of lies! I've been there. Believe me, there are no gators or avalanches or great dismal swamps . . ."

A horseman came picking his way out of the damp green shadows. It was Harry Curry. He reined in, looking down at Matt with sharp concern.

"Are you all right?" he asked. "We were afraid you'd been killed."

"Harry! I thought you were with the advanced party."

"I was . . . while it lasted. We went as far as a place called Great Meadows and started to dig a supply dump. Then my men decided to decamp." Harry shrugged. "There wasn't any point in sitting out there in the middle of nowhere by myself, so I returned to Wills Creek."

"Well, but why did they decide to desert?"

Harry looked at him oddly. "They'd heard a rumor evidently that Washington planned to leave us there on our own for the French to find."

Matt couldn't believe the things he was hearing. "Harry, Harry, where are all these wild rumors coming from? Who's starting them?"

Harry shook his head. "I wouldn't know, Matt. All I know is that this army is mighty unhappy. They seem to feel they're being sold out . . . walked into a trap."

"This is insane!" Matt fumed impotently. "Listen, is Tram back?"

"Yes, days ago."

"Maybe he's the one. Maybe—" But why? Matt wondered. To what end? Tram was a provincial, a Virginian, a militia officer. Why . . .

A great bawling voice boomed down the path.

"Who's that I see down there? Ain't that Matty? Ain't that Matt Burnett I see?"

And a moment later Matt was wrapped tightly in the huge sweaty embrace of Shad Holly, all breezy, beefy, and blatant with happiness.

"Why you fellas bullyraggin' this boy with questions?" he roared at the vanguard. "Can't you see he's beat to a standstill? Matty, you been eatin' regular? You look kind a peeled down to me."

Harry's cutting voice spoke over their heads. "We're all

98

glad to see Matt safely back, but we'd better save the re-union celebration till later, don't you think? I believe we have work to do."

Shad blinked at Harry and blew out his breath. "Well, who's stopping you from getting it done? Do you need me to hold your hand?"

Harry drew himself up in the saddle and turned to Matt again.

"Welcome back, Matt." Then he spoke to the three men of the vanguard. "Let's get on with it, men." He swung his horse away carefully and the three scouts fell into his wake in sullen silence.

Shad lowered his voice somewhat. "See that hoss Harry's got? It's the same nag Cap'n Stephen give him the day we jined up. Harry ain't hardly been out a the saddle since. Thinks he's some kind a officer when he's on a horse." He paused and pursed his lips thoughtfully.

"Funny thing is, most the men seem to think so too."

"Yes," Matt said, understanding it. "It's in his manner. Must get it from his father." Then he put Harry aside. "Shad, what's been going on with this army? These fantastic rumors of gators and avalanches and tidal waves—"

Shad nodded grimly. "Ain't you heard the one about the ravine a mountain lions we got to cross? Oh my yes, it's awful! There's this twenty-mile-long ravine, see? And it's fifty foot deep and fifty foot wide and a couple thousand cougars live in it and . . ." He threw up his skillet-sized hands, shaking his head.

"I dunno, Matty," he said wearily. "They start some-wheres, and they get worse'n worse. Trouble is, none a these fellas has ever been west of the Allegheny before. And after what we've been through getting over that blame mountain, they're ready to believe anything!"

"Has it been bad, Shad?"

"BAD!" The big fellow fairly exploded the word. "Listen,

99

Matty, you know this Injun path—it's so bad the deer won't even use it for a run. And it's the best there is! You know what it's like to shove a hundred'n fifty men up and down a mountain through woods as thick as a brickyard, and hauling wagons and nine cannons? And in the rain?

"Matty, we've chopped down enough trees to make a log town as big as Alexandria! We've bridged streams, thrown up causeways over marshes, pried up rocks no bigger than elephants, and . . ." He stopped, getting his breath, and eyed Matt angrily.

"Yeah, and while I'm talking about this road we been building, I'll tell you another rumor that's just started. Tammy heard it and blacked the eye of the fatmouth who told him. It's going around now that I picked out this path deliberate. You want a know why? Because I want to hold the army back as long as I can. Yeah. And you want a know why I want to hold 'em back? 'Cause I'm in the pay of the French!"

Matt couldn't believe it. "My God, Shad, nobody would believe that! Why, it's incredulous! Who would start a filthy rumor like that?"

Shad shrugged his burly shoulders. "Beats me, Matty. But it's started just the same."

"Have you talked to Washington?"

Shad became animated. "Talk to him! All I ever see of him is a flash here, a zip there. Matty, that boy has his hands full! He's receiving runners, he's writing dispatches, he's sending out wampum belts, he's down to his boot tops in the mud trying to pry loose a bogged cannon, he's doctorin' the sick, he's up at the front seeing what lies ahead, he's at the rear trying to boost along the afterguard. He never sleeps, never eats . . . I tell you, the recording angels who try to keep up their books on that man got to work late and early!"

"All right," Matt said. "I'll talk to him. I've got to report to him anyhow."

The damp woods were very noisy around them now; men's voices, the *tchuk* of axes biting into tree trunks, the tear and catch and rip of falling timber . . . A tall gangly horseman came by them on a sorry-looking spotted nag. He tipped his tri-hat to Shad and smiled dourly.

"*Salve*, Shadrach," he said deeply. He resettled his hat and said, "Hail!" Then he raised his hat again and said, "*Vale*, Shadrach, Meshach, Abednego. Farewell! *Pax vobiscum.*"

Shad grinned after the lanky horseman. "That's Bobby Stobo, a gentleman volunteer. They made him a kind of officer. He's a queer duck, all brains and Latin words. Washington says he's a pal of that English writer Smollett, whoever he is."

An intellectual, a friend of Smollett's, riding a gaunt nag to a war in a howling wilderness. Strange the men war touched; men who belonged somewhere else, doing other things . . . Matt shook his muse and waved to Shad, turning away. "See you, Shad. *Vale!*"

The army was camped down for the night on either side of the road they were hacking out of nature's fortress. They had no tents, no shelter, only the soggy blankets on their backs. Their food was hardtack and what they could scavenge from the woods. But they had water, plenty of water, buckets and rain barrels of it, and they hated it. Was war always fought in the rain and mud? they wondered.

Headquarters had been pitched on a small hardwood ridge overlooking the road. There was one damp tent set among the linden trees and sycamores. Matt reported to Peyroney, requesting to see Washington.

The twenty-two-year-old commander looked thirty-two, a tired thirty-two. He was sitting on a small keg behind a

101

hardtack box. Another officer was with him, Captain Jacob Vanbraam. Matt had heard of the Dutch soldier of fortune; he had been Washington's military tutor. What little Washington knew of warfare he'd learned from Vanbraam.

Washington nodded in reply to Matt's salute, saying, "We'd given you up for lost. Ward returned days ago, and so did his men. Those from your party say you were chased by Mingoes."

"Yes sir. Laurel Ridge Senecas. I escaped from them later. Then I was shagged by some Ottawas. I had to detour."

Washington's look quickened. "Ottawas? That close to Chestnut Ridge?"

"Yes sir. The entire territory west of Chestnut is swarming with hostile Indians. Frenchmen are among them, with war belts."

"Oh? My information from Half King is that Contrecoeur and his army are still at the Forks, building a fort there, called Duquesne."

"The Frenchmen I saw weren't from the Forks, colonel. They were from Venango. Cassanna was with them."

"Cassanna . . . I believe you once said he was a friend of yours."

"Not quite that, sir. I knew him as a boy."

Washington looked at Vanbraam. The Dutchman made swacking noises around the stem of a clay pipe. "Vhy you say Ottavas, poy?" he asked.

"Because they wore horns. That's Ottawa headdress." Backtracking in his mind, Matt realized there was something subtly wrong about this interview. It had the tone of a suspicious investigation. He looked at Washington wonderingly.

"What's so strange about Ottawas being east of the Forks?"

"We have a problem here, Burnett," Washington told

102

him evenly. "There are some weird rumors circulating through this army. As far as I can determine these rumors have a single-mindedness of purpose: to frighten our troops into turning back." His fingers drummed the top of the hardtack box restlessly.

"Our situation is bad. When Ward told me he'd been pushed out of the Forks, I decided that a state of war existed between ourselves and the French, and I ordered the advance, even though Colonel Fry and the rest of the regiment had not reached us.

"Through desertions, sickness, accidents, we are still only one hundred fifty strong. Our supplies are negligible, our ammunition low; we've performed Herculean tasks crossing the Allegheny, and the weather has been inclement to say the least. And now these appalling rumors are starting. You see my point? It wouldn't take much to spook this army into turning back. For instance, if they thought they were going to walk into an Indian ambush at Chestnut Ridge . . ."

"Colonel, are you suggesting that I started these rumors, or had a hand in it?" Matt asked. "Are you saying that I'm lying when I tell you the savages are massing between the Forks and Chestnut?"

Washington's look was level. "I am not. I'm simply apprising you of the situation. Someone in our midst is against us. We don't know who; all we can do is study the evidence as it reaches us. There have been rumors concerning you and Shad Holly. Now, shall I ignore these rumors, or shall I consider them? What would you do in my place?"

Matt agreed, reluctantly, that he would consider the rumors.

"Very well. I met you and Holly for the first time last winter, on Slippery Rock Creek, in the company of a Laurel Ridge Seneca. You said you were trapping, though you had no traps or hides in evidence. You admitted you knew Cassanna. Within the hour a Mingo tried to murder me. All right, leaving that, let's come to last month. I sent you to the Forks, and within a few days Tram arrives in a surly panic; a few days later Ward arrives in a worse panic. But you remain behind."

"Because I was chased by Senecas! Ward's men told you that."

"Yes . . . by Laurel Ridge Senecas. Friends of yours and Holly's, aren't they?"

Matt rubbed at his face. "No—I mean, the one called Chief is our friend. But we don't even know the rest of them. Dammit all, colonel, they were going to kill me!"

"But obviously they didn't. And when you finally do return to us, you come with the bad news—dangerous news for our army's ears—that the savages are massing along Chestnut Ridge; though our friend Half King does not support this story."

"But sir, don't you see that Half King is afraid to tell you of the true situation west of Chestnut? He's afraid that you won't come to his aid if you learn of the opposition against you."

"You could have relieved his fears on that point when you talked to him," Washington said quietly. "I am marching on the Forks, and nothing short of battle and defeat will stop me."

Matt nodded impatiently. "I know that, sir. I'm in accord with—"

"Then why did you tell Ward and his men that I must be warned not to come ahead for fear of walking into a French and Indian trap?"

"I didn't mean it that way! I knew you would come; but I knew you should be informed that the French were ready for you when you did."

"But you didn't say that."

"Because there wasn't time! We had Mingoes down our—"

A shout interrupted him. "Rider coming! Wills Creek way!"

Washington sprang up and hurried past Matt to the tent flap. A moment later a mud-spattered messenger came clumping across the ridge saluting as he said, "Fry's at Wills Creek, colonel, with the rest of the regiment."

"At last!" Washington cried. "How soon can he reach us?"

"Ain't no way a telling, colonel," the rider said. "You see, he's sick. Bad sick. He can't march."

No one said anything for a moment. Officers had gathered around the tent entrance and they watched Washington expectantly. Ward was there (he nodded to Matt) and Tram too. It was Tram who finally spoke up.

"Better forget it, George. We only got three companies. Fry ain't never gonna get here with the other three, and that fool Mackay from South Ca'lina with his hundred regulars ain't neither. By crinkus, we can't fight the French'n Injuns with only a hunnerd'n fifty men!"

In later years history would record that Washington was known for his coolness of judgment, his profound sense of public duty, and strong self-control. But on this wet night in Nemacolin's Path he was barely twenty-two and his rampant nature was aflame with military ardor. He'd been chomping at the bit long enough. Now he spat it out.

"You may do as you please," he told Tram. "Follow me or run for home. I'm marching on Duquesne."

It was the first of May.

Because of the excessive rains and the nature of the terrain, it seemed to the Virginians that the entire wilderness was afloat; that is, the trees and thickets and rocks and craggy ridges were afloat, the underfoot was simply submerged.

The bogs were endless. They dug causeways and laid corduroy roads to cross them. The ravines were as numerous

105

as the wrinkles on an old old Indian's face—clogged with underbrush, treacherous with sheer shaly banks, water-slick rocks. Horses snapped their fetlocks in them, wagons dropped their wheels, men twisted their ankles. Sometimes a leg was broken, or an arm, or a head . . .

A tunnel had to be hacked through the forest. Axmen beavered the trees close to the ground, leaving stumps with just enough clearance for the undercarriage of wagons, cannons . . . the trees themselves were toppled to the right and left, into the saplings and scrub, creating a double abatis. Streams had to be bridged. Boulder traps for wheels had to be removed.

It rained and rained and rained.

One day was like another: dig, wade, climb, chop, pry, shove, and always, inexorably it seemed, that goshawful eroded gully known as Nemacolin's Path twisted on on on ahead of them, until men began to tell one another that Nemacolin hadn't been an Indian at all. No, it was a blame lie. Nemacolin had been a snake, and for some fool reason or other the snake had wanted to go to the Youghiogheny. None of the Virginians could figure out why; must have been out of its head!

There was very little food. Hunters went out each day to shoot dinner on the hoof or wing. Moccasins were wearing paper-thin, deerskin garments were turning to tatters from the bouts with the saw-bladed swamp grass and bramble thickets, blankets were always soggy, and if you were fool enough to get yourself sick it was just too bad for you. There was no doctor and what you would find in the medicine chest was a laugh . . . if you had the strength to.

Squatting under the drooling pines at night, with a few sticks and leaves and twigs for a fire, Matt talked about the march with his friends. Tammy was there, and Shad and Stefen, and Shad's new friend, Robert Stobo.

106

"What makes them endure it?" he asked. "What makes them go on?"

"Well, it ain't the eightpence a day Virginia's paying 'em. I can tell you that!" Shad said. "Nor the no-pence a day Pennsylvania's paying us. Ain't no man dumb enough to go through this for eightpence!"

"Pro patria," Stobo said simply. "For country."

"Is that it?" Stefen wondered. "For England?"

"I didn't say that," Stobo objected. "Look around you. Where are the Englishmen? I'm talking about the born-in-England-come-here-just-for-the-expedition Englishmen. There are none. Instead you see only provincials. Virginians and Pennsylvanians. Men of this country, this land." He put a hand down and pressed it to the porous earth.

"What of yourself?" Matt asked him. "You're an Englishman."

Stobo grinned. "What is that Mingo word you use? *De'osthon?* Not even a little. I'm a Scotty, and I'm not here to help the King."

"Why, then?" Tammy asked.

"Because this is a new beginning, a new second step for mankind. Because this land has horizons. Because this war we are going to will decide which nation you men of America will later fight for your independence. If France wins, then one day you and Matt and Shad and Stefen will fight France for your freedom. If England wins, then you will fight her for the same reason." He looked at them brightly.

"Don't you see? It is in you, in your roots, to do this thing. It is a need. And it is as inevitable as night following day. It will come."

It will come. The words echoed in Matt's ears. Fight England? Independence . . . maybe . . . maybe so. *Pro patria!*

The march dragged on. One, two, three weeks. Then the west side of Laurel Ridge . . .

107

Great Meadows was not very great, in Shad's estimation.

"A peewit of a place," he told Matt. "A rabbit trap. And wouldn't you know that fool of a Harry would pick such a spot to dump the supplies in! And speaking of 'em, where are the supplies?"

No one knew. They were gone, stolen, presumably. Matt wandered over to the cluster of officers talking in the meadow. Washington seemed to accept the blow as a trick of war. He was casual about it.

"It's no good trying to foist the blame on Curry, gentlemen. What would you have done in his boots? His men ran off on him taking all the horses save one. He couldn't transport the abandoned supplies by himself, and it would've been foolhardy to remain here on guard alone."

"Well, I would've!" Shad muttered behind Matt's back. And Matt, though he said nothing, believed the big fellow would have at that.

"Well, what are we gonna do?" Tram growled. "No supplies, no fort, not enough men to fight our way out of a paper bag. I say go back! Before we all get ourselves killed!"

Washington shook his head. "No. We will wait here for Colonel Fry's companies. When they arrive, we will attack."

"And if they don't arrive?"

Washington smiled thinly. "Then we will let the French attack." He turned away with Vanbraam at his elbow, saying lightly, "A charming field for an encounter, don't you think?"

Matt felt the way Shad did about the meadow: it was too small, too confined. It was a level tract of weed and scrub, traversed by a long jagged gully like an erratic knife slash on the belly of the clearing. Low wooded hills going on around hemmed the meadow in. Four miles away stood the lofty green ridge of Laurel Hill.

Washington ordered the Virginians to encamp. Then he put them to work clearing the bushes and turning the traverse ditch into an entrenchment. Scouts were sent out, hunters, and a messenger was dispatched to Wills Creek and on to Dinwiddie. An air of urgency was settling over the little army.

Too urgent for Captain Tram . . .

The captain and his little gang of backwoodsmen decided to leave. They departed sullenly, stubbornly, and with a hangdog look about them. The loyal Virginians hooted and jeered them all across the meadow and into the woods, Shad Holly leading the jeerers and doing most of the hooting. You could hear him even out of sight.

"Oh, Mother, Mother, help me quick! I've dropped my hanky! Whatever sh-all I do? Here! You boys be careful with them muskits! What if one of 'em went off by accident? You want a scare poor li'l Cap'n Tram and his bully boys clear back to the Atlantic shore? That's a long run—even for frightened little girls! Oh-oh! Scatter, girls! A one-legged half-blind eighty-year-old Catawba squaw is hobblin' down the path after you! HI-YYYYY-YI!"

The following morning a friendly Seneca came trotting into the meadow. He was from Half King and he bore a message. Washington called his officers together and told them the news.

"The French have marched from their fort. They mean to attack the first English they shall meet. I believe they must have us in mind."

10

THE SHOT THAT SET
THE WORLD ON FIRE

Christopher Gist, according to Shad, was either the bravest or dumbest man alive. Early that spring he had gone into the Mingo and Delaware territory and built himself a trapper's cabin, fifteen miles north of Great Meadows.

Gist, trapper, surveyor, scout, was known by most of the Indians and even respected by many; but still, it seemed a chancy place and time to build a house. "Like sitting on a seam-sprung keg of gunpowder with a torch," was Shad's opinion.

Two days after the arrival of Half King's runner, Gist rode into the meadow on a well-lathered horse. There was an urgency of excitement about him that prompted Matt to suspect that Gist's personal powder keg had finally gone off.

It nearly had.

"George!" Gist shouted breathlessly. "French! Fifty

Frenchmen were at my cabin last night! They were gonna burn me out, but two of their Mingoes were Genesee friends of mine."

"Are they from Duquesne?"

"Yeah. Contrecoeur sent 'em. A Coulon de Jumonville, an ensign, is in charge. This Jumonville claims he's a civil messenger bearing a French summons for you."

"Then why doesn't he simply march in under a flag of truce and deliver it?" Washington demanded.

Gist sneered. "Because I don't think he is a messenger at all. I think Contrecoeur sent him to spy, to determine your strength and fortifications. They're building up for an attack, George!"

Matt had been standing in the background, and now he spoke up.

"Sir, if the French are skulking in the woods, Shad and I could take a party and find them."

There was a marked hesitation in Washington's manner, and Matt noticed that some of his officers were watching him peculiarly. Then Vanbraam broke the awkward silence.

"Hid's a jop for an officer."

Washington nodded abruptly. "Yes. Captain Hoag, take seventy-five men and scour the area."

Matt and Shad returned to the entrenchment and squatted down with their muskets to await developments. They watched Hoag lead half the Great Meadows force into the woods. Matt had nothing to say.

But Shad did.

"You know what that means," he prompted glumly, "when Georgie turned down your offer. It means he still don't trust us."

"It's not his fault, Shad " Matt tried to be empathic about it. "Look at it from his side. Someone started all those vicious rumors, and you and me were included in 'em. Whether he believes the rumors about us are true or not

111

doesn't matter. But if he sent us out in charge of that party and something went wrong . . . you know what his officers and men would think then, don't you?"

"Sure, sure!" Shad raged. "And they're gonna go right on thinkin' it as long's you'n me continue to sit on our fats and never do nothing to prove to 'em how wrong they are!"

Matt nodded. There was something in that, all right.

The search was a waste of time. Hoag returned and reported. "The French have hidden themselves so well that only the eye of an Indian could spot them."

"Next time I'll send an Indian," Washington said irritably.

The strain of waiting was beginning to tell.

Night came in sections. It came creeping under the trees and into the meadow, stretching its shadows farther, farther, until the shadows joined and melted and lost their shape and pattern, and then everything was shadow, and there was no moon.

An Indian, as silent and dark as the night itself, slipped from the woods and stopped at the apron of the meadow. He called to the fireflylike cluster of little campfires.

"Tohne waktan'ha! O'nen ni'a hau!" Here I stand. Now I am coming.

But he wouldn't have come far if it hadn't been for Shad; because the nervous sentry who heard the call didn't know Seneca from Latin and an Indian in the woods at night was an Indian looking for trouble, and he almost let the messenger have a musket ball.

Fortunately, Shad was coming from the creek with a pail of water and he heard the call and saw the sentry throw up his musket.

"Put down that popgun, you flea-bit, misbegot nephew of a toad! Don't you know a friend when you see him? Ain't safe for a man to step off in the bush with the likes a you around!"

The camp was armed and aroused now, as Shad led the

112

Seneca over to the officers' fire. "Another of Half King's boys," he told them. "His name's Silverheels." Then he questioned the brave, translating the answers.

"Is my brother hungry?" This was ceremony, the polite preliminaries. Silverheels patted his firm stomach. "I have eaten. I am full."

"What is the nature of my brother's news?"

"Tanacharison, our *ha'sennowa'nen,* would have his brothers know that his lodge is now but eight musket shots away, and that he has with him six braves. He would have his brothers know that at the time of the sun's death [sunset] I discovered the tracks of two men. Further, that I followed them to a place of sunken darkness in the forest."

"Did my brother in his wisdom know them for Frenchmen?"

"Continue to listen," Silverheels said. "They are indeed Frenchmen. Further, they are a war party of thirty-five Frenchmen."

"That settles it!" Washington said. "Jumonville is playing the part of a spy and enemy to perfection. I advocate prompt action!"

"But they haven't shown their hand yet," Captain Stephen argued. "Suppose they are merely acting as couriers?"

"And suppose a skunk does look like a pretty kitty," Shad shoved his oar in. "Does that mean he won't give you a barrelful if you step on his tail?"

"My fear is this," Washington stated. "Jumonville and Contrecoeur are up to a strategem to surprise our camp. Now, we can sit here and let it happen, or we can go out and do something about it."

Stephen still wanted to pick at it. "My only concern is that if we provoke Jumonville into a fight, we are deliberately causing a war."

"Causing a war!" Shad bellowed. "Ain't what they already done to us causing a war? Didn't they try to murder

113

the colonel here last winter? Didn't they blow Ward and Matt out a the Forks? Didn't they shag 'em and shoot 'em clear down to Chestnut Ridge? Ain't that cause enough? I can tell you it sure would be for me, brother! Sir."

"One moment, Holly," Washington intervened. He turned to Stephen again. "You don't consider what we are in now a state of war?"

"No, sir, I don't. Not officially. And I'm certain the French don't either. The violence to date has been Indian shooting Indian or Indian shooting white man. But if we fight Jumonville, that's Frenchman against Englishman. And that, sir, is official war."

Shad blew out his breath. "Official. Hmm. I never thought a that before. You know, colonel, what we ought a do is send a patrol back along the You River to find them dead'n scalped men of Ward's and tell 'em they ain't really dead . . . not officially, that is. Poor devils have been layin' out there for weeks thinkin' they was dead'n gone, when all the time—" Matt gave the big fellow a hard nudge.

Washington was on his feet now and he looked at his officers with the bright eye of youthful aggressiveness.

"As far as I'm concerned, the seizure of a king's fort by planting cannon against it and threatening it with destruction is a declaration of war on the part of the French. I have little interest as to what history's slant will be on what we decide here and now. Condemned or commended, gentlemen, tonight we attack!"

The rain had started again. It fell from the pitchy sky like black ink, ice cold. Shad was somewhere up ahead with Silverheels and Washington. There hadn't been any question this time about Shad and Matt joining the party. Washington was setting out for Half King's camp with forty men, hoping to persuade his old friend's braves to join the expedition. Interpreters might be needed.

114

Ward was there, and Stobo, and Tammy and Stefen. But Matt had no idea exactly where. It was all he could do to see the back of the Virginian in front of him; the night and woods were that dense.

The path was hardly wide enough for one man and they lost it repeatedly, stumbling blindly over the ground pumpkined with oak roots, through azalea tangles, bumping into each other in the murky dark, muttering, "Who's that? . . . Where are the others? . . . Does anybody know where we're going, for grab's sake?"

"Brother," an undistinguishable man who had fallen in at Matt's side for a few moments murmured, "would you believe I got a five-room house in Philly and three hunnerd dollars in the bank? And lookit me now! Not that you can in this blame tar barrel."

"Are you from Pennsylvania?" Matt wondered.

"Sure. I'm a volunteer just like you. I ain't gonna let these toe-eared Virginians spend the rest a their days crowing how they whipped the frog-eaters!"

Dawn was just preparing to put its shoulder under the lid of the eastern horizon and lift when the party slogged out of the drenched forest and up to Half King's tepees. There was a hurried count of heads. Seven men had been lost in the woods and left behind.

"We're gonna need these Seneca, Matt," Stefen said. "Thirty-three tired men against thirty-five rested ones is poor odds."

"Odds mean little in a war," Stobo said. "Determination is the deciding factor."

Shad strode over to them with all the beefy bluster of a man of great affairs. "Georgie and that bug-eater Half King is holdin' a powwow," he told them importantly. "I guess Georgie don't need me for a minute. He told me to get myself some air. But I told that bug-eater the situation before I left. I said, 'Tanacharison, if you plan on being set down

115

in the white man's history books as a ferocious warrior instead of an old woman who squats around in her wickiup
pickin' lice out a her deerskins, then you'll throw in with
me'n Georgie.' That's what I told him."

Stobo grinned wolfishly at the big fellow. "Shad, Shad.
Whatever would this army do without your bombastic presence?"

"I dunno," Shad said modestly. Then he squinted suspi-
ciously at his lanky friend. "Say, what is bombastic, anyhow?"

Half King, somewhat to Matt's surprise, decided to help
the Virginians, and the march was resumed. Two Senecas
led the way. The tracks of the two French scouts seen the
day before were rediscovered, and the war party formed
two parallel lines and slipped silently into the forest.

There was a halt. Washington and Stephen were convers-
ing in whispers. Stephen was to take the left wing, Washington the right. Matt watched twenty men file off to the left.
Shad was one of them.

The right wing started to move. Word passed down the
line, man to man: "No talking . . . get ready . . . we're close
. . . bay'nets."

Matt drew from his belt the bayonet he'd been issued and
secured it to the end of his musket. He looked at it apprehensively. It was long, slim, brittle-bright. He had never
used one before. A peculiar sense of emptiness cloyed in his
stomach. War, he thought bleakly. In just a minute now—
war. Battle . . .

The party pushed noiselessly up to the brow of a long flat
ledge that looked down into a rocky hollow.

The Frenchmen were gathered in the glen below them,
sitting and milling around their morning fire. Their voices
drifted upward.

"On se trouve bien ici dans la fraîcheur . . ."

Washington held a long-barreled pistol in his hand, and

he looked back from his crouching position near the lip of the rock ledge to fan the pistol at his men, signaling them to deploy along the ledge.

Matt crouched behind Tammy and started crawling through the wet weeds, swinging toward the right. A burly Virginian bumped shoulders with him and they looked at each other startlingly. The Virginian's face was iron-eyed with nervous anticipation. Matt wondered what his own face looked like.

I'm scared, he thought. I honestly am.

He edged by Robert Stobo. The Scotsman's lips were forming soundless Latin words. *Pax vobiscum anno domini* . . . So's he, Matt thought. That made him feel better, somehow. He wondered where Shad and Stefen were. He wondered, absurdly, what his father and the twins were doing at that very minute. He wondered what he'd be doing twenty years from that minute. Or if . . .

It was 8 A.M.

Now he could actually see the Frenchmen, all of them; the ensign, Jumonville, another officer, three very young cadets, and thirty other soldiers. Jumonville was standing by the fire.

Then he looked up, and it seemed to Matt that he looked at him.

"Aux armes! Les Anglais!"

The French went scrambling madly for their arms as Washington stood up, aimed his pistol, and shouted his first combat command.

"FIRE!"

All along the rocky wall a great mushroom of smoke bannered as the muskets went *Ka-bal-lolololowm!* And Matt felt the butt sock in his shoulder as he saw, dimly, Frenchmen jacking over, falling, running, turning to aim upward and fire back. Then the lip of the ledge was going *whock-whock-whock* around him as the return fire spattered on the

117

rocks and went whining off in a ricochet tune . . . *pweeenng*.

Ducking his head, he fumbled in his shot bag for another ball. A Virginian sprawled on his right, with a face that looked as lumpy as a basket of ripe plums, slobbered words at him.

"Min yer mou, moy! Min yer mou!" And, to show him, spat a musket ball from his mouth into his left hand, then rolled over to reload.

A Lieutenant Waggener went over backwards as if he'd been snatched by the scruff of the neck. "What was that?" he yelled at anyone. "What was that?" He had been hit in the arm but didn't seem to realize it.

The Virginians' powder was damp from their long sojourn in the wet night woods, and their next volley was ragged and nearly ineffectual. And now the French were fully armed and their powder was dry and they were chipping away at the brow of the ledge like a woodpecker drilling a hurried hole.

"*Feu! Sangdieu! Feu! Feu!*" Fire.

"*Apportez-moi un aut—*"

Washington seemed to dance along the ledge, stepping between the outflung legs of his men, the bullets skipping and whacking around him, *dok-dok-doking* into the trees behind him. He threw the empty pistol down and snatched out his sword, pointing the blade at the glen.

"CHARGE!"

Matt shoved up, men rising all around him, coming to their feet, screaming, the terror-spreading cry of the Seneca braves going *eeeee-yuyuyu-uuuu!* And somewhere off to the left Shad's sudden HI-YI!

Down the rock face the Virginians and Senecas slithered and leaped and tumbled, and it was sixteen feet sheer if it was an inch and they came down in twisted bouncing clumps, all arms and legs and guns and shouting; Matt going feet-first and then into a sudden sickening tilt as someone, something slammed his left shoulder, and he saw a man rushing up to meet him and crashed into him, then went sprawling head-first across the brilliant wet turf, and struck, skidded, and found himself in a hand-to-hand fray.

He swung his musket up and warded a bayonet thrust from a Frenchman who, in fury, seemed to be all eyes, mustache and screaming mouth. Then someone blundered into the Frenchman and he just seemed to disappear, swallowed in the general confusion.

Right ahead of Matt was Half King and he swung his tomahawk behind his left shoulder and then took one mighty horizontal sweep with it, and that was when Matt saw the Seneca's target. Jumonville went down under the tomahawk as though he'd been poleaxed.

"Cover! Cover!" some fool was yelling.

But it seemed like a good idea to Matt. This bayonet to tomahawk to knife business was downright dangerous! He slid behind a rock and fumbled a ball from his shot bag, dumped powder down the barrel, dropped the ball home (to heck with wadding), gave the butt a slap with the palm of his hand to joggle powder into the pan, cocked, swung the barrel up, and just in time to catch a Frenchman rushing him with a bayonet that looked a yard long.

The musket kicked like a door slamming and the Frenchman came at him in a somersault and stopped all at once against the rock and all topsy-turvy.

Matt turned and saw Ward crawling toward him, sword in hand. His face looked like a grinning mask of skin stretched tightly over bone. His left sleeve was scarlet-bright from a wound.

"You got him, Matt! You got him!"

"By crinkus, we got 'em all!" someone yelled from behind them.

It was true. Everywhere they could hear the French shouting:

119

"Reddition! Reddition! Je rends!" I surrender.

It was over. Matt got up slowly, blinking around at the carnage.

The Virginians were herding the disarmed French into a tight huddle. There were twenty-two of them. Ten besides Jumonville were on the ground for good. One Frenchman had escaped. The Virginians were jubilant.

Half King wanted to scalp the prisoners, but Washington looked at him coldly and said, "Don't be silly." Then he approached Ward, who was letting Stobo attend to the bayonet scratch on his arm, and asked the time-honored, inevitable question that followed all military engagements.

"What's the butcher's bill, ensign?"

"A smashing victory, sir! One for the books. Oh, we have our share of wounded, but we only lost one man!"

The glen rang with the cheers of the Virginians. It was a remarkable stroke of luck.

Then Matt turned and saw Shad and Stefen coming toward him. They had the identical look of men on a sorry mission.

"Matt—" Shad began in a strangely quiet voice. "That one man—Stevie found him. He . . ."

The sun went out for Matt, a wintry sensation blew through his chest. He stared at Stefen vacantly. Stefen nodded.

"Yes, Matt . . . it was Tammy."

The three Pennsylvanians and Stobo buried him in the glen where he had died with his father's claymore in his hand. They were alone in the rocky hollow. Washington, now that the war had "officially" begun, feared another French attack at any moment, and he had vacated the glen immediately with his men and prisoners.

"You don't have much time for ceremony," he warned Matt before departing. "This is war now, and the bones of

120

many men will molder on the earth instead of under it. I'm sorry, but be as quick as you can. We have a fort to build."

Shad thought it would be a nice touch to bury the claymore with Tammy; but Matt said no. He picked it up and set it aside. He was going to take it back to Tammy's father. It was something, at least.

"Bobby," Shad said, "you speak some Latin over him."

But Stobo didn't. Instead he simply said, "Dig not too narrow, not too deep, that I may come forth."

Matt liked that. It gave him a warm feeling, as though Tammy wasn't through with life. Not really.

He followed his friends up a crevice in the wall, then paused to look down into the quiet little glen, at the flat rock at the head of a dirt mound.

"Pro patria," he murmured.

It was the twenty-eighth of May.

11

FORT NECESSITY

So Washington had fired the shot that caused the first world war of modern times; 853,-000 soldiers were to die because of Jumonville's Glen. And more—the obscure skirmish of May 28, 1754, was to open the long, hard contest for the rights of man against the institutions of the feudal ages which had been transplanted to America. It was to shatter the underpinning of Europe's decadent society.

Though, of course, none of that little band of backwoods Virginians, toiling in their ragged clothes in the wet wilderness, knew it at that time.

And then the rumors started again.

Matt had thought that with the departure of Captain Tram this sort of vicious, behind-the-hand undermining would cease. But it didn't. And suddenly there were ugly and false whispers of assassination.

The first Matt knew of it was the morning after the battle in the glen, when Christopher Gist was dispatched with a handful of men and the French prisoners for Wills Creek. He discovered Shad in a fight with two Virginians on the edge of the entrenchment.

Matt ran to assist his friend, but his help wasn't really needed. Shad already had one of the militiamen flat on his back in the weeds and out cold, and the second one, from the way Shad was handing him sledgehammer rights and lefts, was well on his way to joining the first.

"Are you tellin' me, brother?" Shad was bellowing, right-cross to the jaw, left pile driver to the breadbasket. "I was there! Where was you when Georgie'n me was beatin' Frenchies off our backs by the dozen?"

The militiaman must have found the question rhetorical, because by this time he was curled up cozily with his friend in the weeds and he was in no condition to tell Shad where he'd been during the fight in Jumonville's Glen. So Shad told him, hollering over him as he dozed.

"Back here diggin' patty cakes in the mud in this ditch! That's where you was, brother!" Then he swung around and glared fiercely at the cluster of Virginians who had gathered to see the fight.

"That's where you all was!" he roared. "I know you! I know who was with Georgie'n me! And it wasn't none of you!"

"Hit's a blame lie!" a little scrawny fellow with a beard down to his Adam's apple cried. "I was there! I got me one a them cay-dets! And I'll lick the man says I warn't er din't!"

Shad looked at the little pipsqueak as though he'd eat him alive in one gulp. Then he blinked and smiled agreeably.

"I know you was, brother. I recognize you. And I a-pologize for my hasty words. I din't mean to include you with the rest of these turnip-toed, hog-rumped, bat-blind Virginians!"

123

"I'm fum Virginny!" the little fellow snapped. "And I'll lick the man says a word agin her!"

"Brother," Shad said forgivingly, "I ain't holdin' it agin you. I won't tell nobody." Then he turned back to the rest of them. "All right, anybody else want to tell me to my face that Georgie assynated Jumonville in the back?"

The Virginians were growing downright angry; anyone could see they were ready to go to scratch. None of them were foolhardy enough to take Shad on alone, but Matt could see that if Shad didn't stop riling them they'd take him en masse.

He grabbed his big friend's arm and tugged. "Cut it out, Shad. Leave them alone. C'mon!" Slowly, with reluctance on Shad's part, Matt drew him away from the seething crowd.

"What's it all about?" he demanded. "Why were you fighting?"

"Why was I fighting! I'll tell you why was I fighting, and then you'll want to go back there with me and wake them two flatland-stompin' celery-heads up and beat 'em all over agin! I was fighting 'cause them rumpheads that wasn't even there said Washington assynated Jumonville!"

"Now hold on, will you? What is this assynated thing?"

"Assynated? Don't you know what assynated means, Matt? My goodness, ain't you never been to school? Don't you know the ruddyments of the King's English even? Assynate means murder, that's what it means! Yeah, that's what they're trying to pin on Georgie now—murder!"

"You're not serious."

"Ain't I? Ain't I? Ain't I got ears? Them two fellas said to me they heard Jumonville was a civil messenger with a summons from Contrecoeur, and that when Jumonville seen Washington up on the ledge he called out that he had a dispatch for him, but that Washington went right ahead and shot him down in cold blood!"

124

Matt was aghast. "Where did they hear such a tale? It's not true at all! Jumonville looked me right in the face and shouted 'To arms!' "

"Are you tellin' me?" Shad asked. "Wasn't I there? Wasn't I up on that gafocky ledge with Frenchies usin' me as a bull's-eye? And you know what else they ast me? They ast me was it true we then sat up there and shot the unarmed Frenchies down like ducks in a barrel! Unarmed!"

Robert Stobo, however, when Matt told him of the lies he'd heard, didn't seem at all surprised.

"When you're my age, Matt, you'll realize that the really great thing about any great man is that he continues to plow ahead to greatness even though a multitude of little, jealous, inadequate men continually throw hooks and snares at him to hold him back."

Perhaps this was so, because Washington, Matt observed, made no excuses, rebuttals, or comments regarding his actions on the morning of May the twenty-eighth. He plowed ahead with his work, the fortification of Great Meadows.

It was Half King who loudly revealed himself as the Hero of Jumonville's Glen. Pompous, self-important, he strutted around the meadow with Jumonville's scalp on the butt of his tomahawk. Shad mockingly took to calling him "Tanacharison, the Terror of Jumonville's Glen."

It had never been Washington's intention to be besieged at Great Meadows; rather he had planned on meeting the French in the open in the grand old style of the archaic European armies, according to Vanbraam's code of warfare. And, with this premise in mind, the fort, which was actually no more of a fort than Fort Prince George had been, was a lackadaisical affair, a patchwork fort.

Two entrenchments were dug in the shape of right angles, facing in on one another to form a curious quadrilateral with two salients left open. The four sides varied in length

125

from sixty to one hundred feet, and the dirt from these rifle pits had been thrown forward to serve as an earth embankment.

Inside the quadrilateral, and set back in the open northeast salient, was a small log stockade with a diameter of fifty-three feet and a circumference of one hundred sixty-eight feet. The command tent was set up inside this palisade. Overhead floated the red-and-white double cross on a field of blue. The Union Jack.

It was Peyroney who ran it up on a sapling flagstaff, and when he did he said something that stuck in Matt's mind. The ensign looked up at the lazily unfurling flag and then looked at Matt and pointed to the ground.

"No matter what comes, Burnett . . . this spot is England!"

Yes . . . perhaps so; but it was more than that to Matt. It was himself and Ward at the Forks of the Ohio, and his father at Louisburg, and Washington in the Nemacolin Path on the night of May the first, and Shad yelling Hi-yi at Jumonville's Glen, and Chief standing rigorously over him and saying *Then'en* to savages who were his brothers and yet were not. It was Robert Stobo pressing his hand to the earth and saying, "It will come."

It was the Virginians who, without supplies or shelter, had forced a disputed passage over the Alleghenies in witch's weather, and who were now ready to go to scratch.

Washington named the fort with an ironic smile.

"I dub thee Fort Necessity."

Half King and his Senecas moved into the meadow and set up their tepees, along with a curious individual known as the female Potentate, Queen Aliquippa, who smoked a stone pipe and wore ratty-looking old scalps around her waist, and who hailed from the head of the Mon. (The Terror of Jumonville's Glen's girlfriend, Shad called her.) With her came some thirty Indian families.

Then Gist returned with the news that Colonel Fry was dead, and Washington succeeded officially to the command of the regiment.

Next to make an appearance at Great Meadows was a Major Muse with the three remaining companies that had been under Fry's command, and Washington's rank and file had suddenly doubled in number.

And finally, toward the end of June, Captain Mackay's company of regulars arrived from South Carolina, and the little army had swollen to four hundred strong.

Great Meadows was suddenly an animated camp.

But there was friction. Captain Mackay presented himself to Washington with jovial courtesy, commended the young commander's Virginians for their courage and endurance, and then swung around to the point that was uppermost in his mind.

"I understand that you are a militia officer, colonel?" he said, smiling genially.

"That's correct."

"And, of course, you realize that I hold my commission from the King?" Mackay prompted.

"Yes, but I fail to see——"

"What I'm getting at, colonel, is that it would not be seemly for me to be under orders to a mere—nothing personal, you understand—to a mere militia officer. No, no, not seemly at all. My men—regulars, all of them—wouldn't understand, wouldn't appreciate it."

Washington stared at the commander of the regular company. All of his officers stared at the amiable, courteous holder of the King's commission. What in the devil was the man getting at?

Mackay smiled at them. "We understand one another then, eh?" he asked. Washington shook his head.

"My apologies, captain . . . but I'm afraid we don't."

Mackay raised an eyebrow. "You don't? I thought I made

127

it plain enough. Very well, if you insist, I'll put it bluntly: I cannot take orders from you."

"Captain, are you suggesting that I relinquish my command to you?" Washington asked quietly.

"No no no, nothing that unorthodox!" Mackay hastened to assure him. "A colonel, even a militia colonel, under a captain would be too preposterous. What I'm suggesting is a joint command."

"A joint command? You and I?"

"Precisely!"

"I'm sorry, captain," Washington said, with grave courtesy, "but I fear I cannot accept your generous offer. That sort of arrangement never works out. It causes nothing but confusion and chaos."

Mackay looked at him blandly. "You refuse then?"

"My apologies, captain. I'm afraid I must."

Mackay smiled a cherub smile. "I see. Well then, I'm afraid there is only one course open for me to take. My men and I will have to remain an independent company."

"You refuse to cooperate?"

"Certainly not, colonel!" Mackay said airily. "We'll cooperate, as long as you comply with the King's regulations. My men will require an additional shilling a day, per man. Otherwise . . ."

Washington's passionate temper almost overruled his patience.

"That is impossible! For one thing we don't have the money to pay it. But even more pertinent, it would breed discontent in my Virginians. Don't you realize, captain, that my men are working and fighting for eightpence a day?"

Mackay dismissed the trifling sum with a wave of his hand.

"But they are only militia, my dear colonel. My men are regulars."

128

Washington quelled the angry murmur that came from his officers with a sharp look. Then he turned back to Mackay. His cool politeness was a masterly example of self-control.

"I regret, captain, that I cannot comply with your request."

For the first time Mackay's genial manner dissolved. He rose from his camp stool stiffly.

"Very well. Now, I believe, we understand each other completely. I will not take your orders, nor will my men be subject to them. I bid you good day, gentlemen."

Washington's officers clustered around him like a horde of angry wasps. "You should have kicked the rotter out, sir!" "His military drones will demoralize our men, colonel!" "Place the pompous bummer under arrest, George!"

Washington held up his hand for silence.

"Gentlemen, everything you say is true. I would heartily enjoy kicking him out of camp; I would love to turn him over to the provost marshal; but, the tragic truth is we need him and his company.

"We have suffered desertion, sickness and death. Our Virginia force is now down to two hundred and fifty men. If the reports we receive from friendly Indians are true, we will shortly go into battle against a vastly superior force of French and Indians. Don't you see? We must have Mackay's one hundred regulars!"

But the situation grew more intolerable with each passing day. Mackay and two ensigns sat by themselves in a little tent off to one side of the clearing and refused to have anything to do with the militia officers. And the South Carolina regulars refused to do a lick of work.

They lazed around the meadow and picked their ears and made themselves obnoxious to the hardworking Virginians in general. The only time they actually had to make a physical effort was when they would get into a fistfight with one

129

or more of the irate militiamen. And usually it was Shad they had to fight.

"How many of 'em did you say there was?" he asked Matt. "A hunnerd? Umm. That only leaves me eighty some to go. I only hope them frog-eaters'n Mingoes hold off till I get the job done!"

Then he asked Matt if he'd heard that Mackay wouldn't even accept the countersign from Washington.

"By grab, it's true!" he cried wrathfully. "And if you think that don't make a hoppin' hades of a mess on the picket line at night, you're coo-coo!

"Stevie was coming back from a scout last night and he ran into some dogface Ca'lina regulars on sentry-go and he had to stand out there in the woods for ten minutes shoutin' the password at 'em, which they didn't know, while they made up their minds if they should fire a volley into him! Dumb, lice-chasin', katniss-eatin' peebrains!"

Matt was concerned that Shad would go too far in provoking the worthless regulars; and the following day his fears were confirmed. He and Shad were ordered to report to the CO's tent.

Washington was there, as well as Captain Mackay and Ensign Peyroney, and Harry Curry, too. Washington addressed Shad blandly.

"Holly, Captain Mackay has brought charges against you for molesting his men."

"Molesting 'em, colonel?" Shad said. "Naw, it ain't true. I call 'em leather-headed pigs, which is the truth; and if they're standing around in my way when I'm trying to do some work, I kick 'em to heck aside; and if they object any to that, I push in their noses and pound 'em on their empty heads and boot their fat backsides up around their ears . . . but I don't molest 'em none, colonel."

Mackay turned to Washington without his usual air of geniality.

130

"Mr. Curry here was witness to one of these disgusting incidents this morning, colonel. Mr. Curry affirms that he was present when this big bruiser deliberately provoked one of my men into a fight . . . a fight which, I might add, cost my man two front teeth."

Washington turned to Harry. "Mr. Curry?"

Harry had not once looked Matt in the face. He stared dispassionately at Shad.

"The regular in question was minding his own business, when Holly called him a 'pig-stealing, slew-footed, shovel-faced toad,'" Harry stated calmly. "He, Holly, further asserted that any man from Carolina with a wart on his chin didn't have the courage to fight a fly if the fly weighed more than an eighth of an ounce. When the regular—who happened to have a wart on his chin—objected to this public slander, Holly knocked him down."

"Is that all I called him?" Shad wondered, with a look of disbelief. "Are you sure I didn't call him a shiftless, bent-eared, hook-nosed, misbegat son of a—"

"That will do nicely, Mr. Holly," Washington said smoothly. "You may answer the charge if you choose."

"Bet your best boot I choose, colonel! That dogface regular was standing on top of a ditch me'n three Virginians was diggin'. I mean he was just standin' there doing nothing! Watchin' us work. And when I said to him 'Will you kindly hand me that pick by your foot, brother, so I can go on digging and you can go on yawning and watching me?' he said no, he wasn't takin' no orders from no Virginia oaf.

"Now, colonel, I didn't mind being called a Virginian; but ain't no man gonna call me a oaf! That's when I called him all them names. And when he 'objected,' like Curry says, he done it by reachin' for his bay'net. That's when I clumb out a the ditch and trounced him, somewhat."

"I've heard of you, Holly!" Mackay said warmly, pointing a finger at Shad. "And your friend there, too. You're

131

both palsy-walsy with the Mingoes! Maybe you can pull the wool over the colonel's eyes, but if I were in command here I'd either have you shot as traitors or drummed out of camp for consorting with the enemy!"

Matt wanted to step around the hardtack box and ram the words down Mackay's fat mouth. Washington, however, intervened sharply.

"That will do, captain! These men have not been brought here to answer a charge of collusion. The circulating rumors regarding them have never been substantiated."

"They haven't been disproved, either," Mackay said sulkily.

"Regardless of that," Washington snapped, "in my book a man is innocent until proven guilty. We'll say no more about it." He turned to Shad and Matt.

"There is enough inner strife in this army without you stirring up more, Holly. I believe your intentions are well meant, but their results can prove disastrous. I'm not placing you under arrest, but I am placing you under restraint. Burnett here is going to be responsible for your explosive temper.

"Do you understand, Burnett? He's your friend. It's your duty to keep him out of trouble. If I hear that he's provoked another regular into a fight, you'll both be under arrest. Dismiss!"

In the chill misty night Matt tossed fretfully in his blankets. He was alone in the drafty camp shed, a shallow little lean-to he shared with Shad, and the dark parade of ominous thoughts that marched through his brain with clashing hobnailed boots refused him sleep.

He didn't blame Washington for the line of action he had taken that day; it was essential that Washington maintained a sense of harmony in his little army, otherwise they were all lost and defeated before the first shot was fired.

132

And his method of restraining Shad's bombastic temper had been a shrewd move. Matt was Shad's best friend and Shad wouldn't endanger their friendship by any untoward action that would place Matt under arrest.

But still, their situation was intolerable. As long as the slightest stigma of doubt hung over them they were not free men. They were under question, and the shadow of it would dog them all their lives.

He felt certain that someone had used him as a cat's-paw, a tool to serve that unknown someone's devious purpose. Someone had frightened Tram away from the Forks and thrown doubt into Ward's mind regarding Washington's intentions. Someone had frightened the advance supply party into deserting and had thrown doubt into Harry's mind, again regarding Washington's intentions.

And he, Matt, had just happened to be alone in the vicinity when it occurred. And because Shad was his friend and because both of them were the friends of a Laurel Ridge Seneca and because all three of them had been present when another Seneca tried to murder Washington, he and Shad had become the scapegoats for the rumor-spreading.

"But who?" he asked the mute night. "Who is doing it?"

He heard the *thup-thup* of feet coming his way, and then the burly silhouette of Shad Holly loomed into a squat at the open end of the lean-to. Shad took Matt's right foot and shook it.

"You awake, Matty? Get your muskit and shot bag. We're getting out a here."

Matt sat up, staring at the bulky black shape of his friend.

"Getting out? What do you mean?"

"I mean we're gonna slip through the picket line tonight. Now."

"Have you gone mad? That's desertion!"

"No it ain't. I got my gorget and you got Tammy's sword, ain't you? That means we're the officers of the Pennsylvania

133

company, don't it? Well, I'm assigning me to special duty and you to help me carry it out. That don't sound like desertion to me."

"No, it sounds like double talk." Matt was beginning to suspect that Shad's mind had gone twirly. "Why would you want to go running off for the woods? What can you gain by that?"

"Because Chief's out there," Shad told him impatiently, "and he's waitin' for me, and because I can't take off on my own 'cause if I do Washington will toss you into quod.

"Listen, Matty, there's gonna be a powwow on the You River, and I think we better sit in on it. Because, among other things, I think we'll find out who's been knifin' you'n me'n Georgie and the whole army in the back."

Matt sat all the way up. He grabbed Shad's thick shoulders.

"How? How can we find out, Shad?"

"Listen, you remember them deserters that run out on Harry? Well, one of 'em didn't make it. The Laurel Ridgers caught him. He's still alive, Matty, thanks to Chief mostly, and he's been telling that old bug-eater something. Didn't Ward tell you that the man who came to the Forks and got Tram all spooked was a tanned man with a beaver cap pulled low on his head?"

"Yes . . . so?"

"So the reason he was 'tan' was because he wasn't a white man, not full white. And the reason he wore his cap low was so the Virginians wouldn't see his shaved Abenaki topknot. Matty, Chief thinks that man was Cassanna."

12

CASSANNA

Shad had led the way north for two miles to a sheltering stand of chestnuts, where they found Chief and another old Seneca hunkered in cross-legged composure by a small fire. They were smoking their stone pipes placidly, and they grunted at the arrival of the two white men.

Chief shook hands with Matt and said, "Fine!"

"This is Siotee, the Laurel Ridgers' *ne Shadodiowe'-go'wa.*" Shad flicked a fat finger at the Seneca medicine man. "Chief's been hauling him around for a couple of days. They come down from their village to find me, and now they're gonna cross the ridge for the powwow on You River."

Matt looked at the *ne Shadodiowe'go'wa* and thought that he would indeed require "hauling around." He was incredibly old. He looked old enough to be Chief's great-grandfather, and maybe he was.

In the firelight Siotee's brown face looked as worn out

135

and mournful as an old dried prune. It was so crosspatched with wrinkles that the old fellow's obsidian eyes seemed to peer out through a mesh of dark delicate cobweb. He appeared to be studying Matt with great curiosity.

"Ne Seneca haksa'dase'a then'en dion'dak," he said in a stately manner. "A man of the Seneca does not lie. Truly you must be a god, brother. For you have faced *ne Hanisheonon'ge* and yet you live."

"He's heard how you climbed up to the Evil One's cave, Matty," Shad explained. "All the Laurel Ridgers think you're a god now . . . except Chief. Chief knows better. Chief's a Christian. Ain't you, you old fraud?"

Chief nodded with stone-face composure. *"Na'e,* it is even so. Hallelujah, amen!" he said sincerely.

Siotee looked at Chief with marked disapproval. He did not believe in Christianity. He knew better. *Manitou,* God, had created the earth and *ne Eia'dagen'tci,* the grandmother of the earth, had been the mother of a girl man-being, and this girl had been the mother of twins. That was the Seneca version of Genesis and anyone who didn't believe it was a misguided fool. He grunted contemptuously and puffed his pipe.

"I'll tell you what that climb of yours did, Matty," Shad said. "I just found out from Chief tonight. It made them Laurel Ridgers change their minds about fighting for the French."

"You mean they'll fight on our side now?" Matt asked eagerly.

Shad looked covertly at the pipe-sucking Siotee. "That's what the powwow's all about. Delegates from the Shawnees, Delawares, Catawbas and Cherokees are coming to have Siotee make big medicine and decide for 'em. But I can tell you one thing I found out from Chief already . . . Half King's out. He ain't gonna fight for Georgie, nor his braves

136

neither. He ain't sayin' nothing, but you watch. That boy is gonna pull stakes!"

"Are you sure? How does Chief know?"

Shad shrugged and looked at the fire with a glum expression.

"I dunno, Matty. Injuns have a way of foreseeing what's coming. And Chief says Half King is gonna let Georgie down."

They reached the rendezvous in the afternoon of the following day. It was an old burnt-out Shawnee town which had been destroyed in the French and Iroquois War. Matt and Shad and their two Indian friends were the first to arrive.

It was tragic ground, the gray wet sky hulking overhead, a dreary beech grove going on around, a weedy clearing littered with charred ruin. The leaning ridge pole in the decayed council lodge pointed like an accusing finger toward the overgrown path which, once, had resounded with the boots and musket volleys of the soldiers who had come to sack and kill and burn.

But it all belonged to the past, and Matt and Shad and Chief were concerned with the present. The future was in Siotee's gnarled hands.

The aged medicine man lost no time. Realizing that the Indians who had been invited to the powwow were tardy, he grumbled *"Tago aween"* complainingly (never quick, never on time), and went to work to make big medicine.

Chief constructed a little stone hearth for Siotee; over it he built a frame with saplings and covered it with their blankets. Then he made a fire on the hearth and waited until the stones were burning to the touch. Next he swept the fire out and boiled water in an old kettle he'd found in the ruins, and poured the water over the stones.

Siotee, naked and ghastly looking, crawled inside the

137

steam hut and baked himself until the war paint ran from his skin and the wax melted in his ears. (Shad thought there was supposed to be something about Siotee throwing himself into the ice-cold river next; but Siotee was much too old for this extreme measure.) He stumbled from the hut, Chief throwing a blanket over him and helping him to stumble, and then Chief went off to pluck leaves from the "drink bushes."

He concocted a most appalling brew which permeated the clearing with its overpoweringly rank odor and must have tasted like dead skunk, which Siotee proceeded to drink relishingly, saying *Uh! Uh!* and which gave him a frightening case of the dizzies and made him vomit and retch for five straight minutes. Watching him with horror, Matt and Shad began to feel the same way.

But Siotee was now purified. It was time for *ne Shadodiowe'go'wa* to speak with the grandfathers and behold the future.

"If I'd been purified like that," Shad whispered, "it'd be time for me to join the grampaws."

Chief built a podium of stones and covered the top of it with pine cones. Siotee then rooted into his medicine bag and brought forth wondrous things—a deer's heart, frog's intestines, and lumps of sweet gum. He put them with the pine cones. Then Chief spread dry twigs over the magical properties and kindled a fire in the twigs.

Siotee faced south and fanned the fire with a shoddy old eagle's wing.

"*O, ho,*" he said. "*O, ho, ho.*"

His voice was low, slow, sad almost. It seemed not quite a voice at all. It seemed to drift ghostlike across river, forest and mountain. It seemed to backtrack into Indian time.

The fire consumed the deer heart and gum, and Siotee placed tobacco leaves on it and a pungent-sweet smoke drifted away. He fanned.

138

"O, ho," he said sadly. *"O, ho, ho."*

And then he drew a conch shell from his bag and blew on it and the hollow note followed the sad chant and the ghostly smoke. It echoed back quietly. And suddenly Matt felt that he was divorced from time, out of it, and a vivid pageantry stood before him, or perhaps in him . . . Indians watching the strange ships of the Dawn Land people coming for the first time, and the Cross and the cannon, and the false treaties and the land grants for a handful of sparkling beads, and all the smiling promises never kept.

Then the tomahawk and the arrows *ssswitting* in the brush, and cabins burning and war paint flashing down leafy paths, and the scalping knife raised. Then the muskets and uniforms and the hunting grounds devastated, and the red men moving west, always west.

And last, a lone old Indian, tribeless, standing under the setting sun on a far-off nameless prairie, with dead grass and the bleached skulls of war ponies at his feet . . . *O, ho. O, ho, ho* . . .

Siotee blew the conch shell. It shattered in his hands. The grandfathers had answered.

Siotee lowered his arms, letting the fragments of the shell spill from his hands. He walked quietly away and hunkered down before the char-black old lodge, the skeletal rib poles rising starkly behind him. Chief stood by the smoldering stone podium and stared emptily at the ground. Matt knew the answer without Shad telling him.

"C'est finny, as the frog-eaters would say—it's over," Shad said heavily. "Oh, they'll talk about it and argue it over and make great speeches about it, but all of them bug-eaters will know they ain't gonna fight for Georgie."

Matt nodded. "It means we've lost all our Indian allies."

"That's it. The Virginians and regulars are on their own now."

139

"Listen, Shad, what about this captive the Senecas have? Does Chief know where he is?"

"Sure. They got him up at Chief's village. He's just a kid, maybe sixteen. Sometimes they keep 'em when they're young like that; adopt 'em into the tribe or keep 'em as slaves."

"And the Laurel Ridge braves are due here at any minute," Matt said, his mind running ahead of his words. "And that means there'll only be kids and old men and women in the village."

Shad gave him a suspicious look. "What're you playing with?"

Matt wasn't playing with it any longer. He'd made up his mind.

"You and Chief are going to sit in on the powwow and stretch it out as long as you can. I know you can't change their minds, just keep arguing to gain time. I'm going to Laurel Ridge and find that boy."

He ran until nightfall, and then he had to call it quits and grab a few hours' sleep. He'd been on the go for twenty-four hours straight and now he was dead on his feet.

He selected a little clearing with a sumac clump and crawled into it, hopeful that he wouldn't discover he was sharing the bush with a rattlesnake. He ate some Indian corn and jerky and then went to sleep like a dog. But not for long. An hour or so before midnight he was awake and on his way again. It was a trick of the hunted: run by night, sleep by day.

It was fifty miles to the Laurel Ridge village—crow's flight. It was a good bit more when you had feet instead of wings. He trotted quietly along, maintaining a steady rhythmical pace. He was carrying a shot bag, powder horn, grubsack, knife, tomahawk, and musket. It was all he needed. There was plenty of water along the way.

140

At dawn he saw the high hogback of Laurel Ridge humping before him.

That's when the war party jumped him.

There were ten of them and he didn't see them in the dawny dark until the first arrow went *sss-wit* over his left shoulder, and even then—Matt ducking, spinning to the left, taking off on a new track—they were only dusky silhouettes springing from the timber, until one of them let loose an ear-piercing screech.

"Kedmedaagik!" Kill!

Abenakis, he thought wildly. St. Francis Abenakis!

He got out of there in a hurry, leaping fleetly along, bounding over rough ground, watching it scamper toward him; turf right, dirt left, mind the rocks right foot . . . turf, turf, turf . . . shale on the left . . .

A musket went *plamm!* behind him and he dodged for a sugarbush of ratty trees.

The Abenakis thought the world of torture. They tied you to a tree and stripped you and traced a deep circle around your stomach with the point of a knife and let you marvel at the wonders of your own innards. Or they separated the ribs from your backbone and pulled them through the skin and hung you by them to a branch. Or they cut out your tongue and forked it on a stick and set it in front of you as they held your face to a fire and you could stare at your tongue until your eyes boiled over. They were as cute as kittens.

As he darted through the sugarbush he spotted a game trail and he pulled off his powder horn and pitched it toward a witch's hobble at the edge of the run. He looked back as he ran. The horn had hung up on a branch of the hobble and it was bobbling there in plain sight.

It wasn't much of a ruse, but it would slow them for a moment when they saw the horn. They'd wonder, Did he take the game trail? And they'd pause to check for tracks.

Then they'd come on again. He knew it, but every moment he gained was better than gold, a ton of gold.

There was a bit of a drop in the earth ahead of him, a yard of shale, a trickle of amber creek, and a fronting of bracken on the far bank. He ran at it, leaped high and wide, rising over the shale and the flash of water, and came down in the ferny brake and tossed his shot bag to the right where it would dangle in the bracken.

It would take them a bit longer to find his tracks this time.

He heard a whoop on his right and had to turn left again. They were forcing him away from the ridge, herding him north. But that was all right, as long as it wasn't too far north.

Now there was a rise ahead—gentle, turfy, a long gradual slope running up to a break between two overhanging ledges. The break was jammed with fat old lichenous boulders. It looked like a little rock fortress. Perfect.

He went up the run and piled over the moss-damp rocks and into a snug little hollow, faced around in a crouch, palm-slapped a speck of powder into the pan, and leveled his musket down the path.

A minute passed glacierlike. Then he heard the *thupthupping* of the head runner. Then he saw him—barechested with shocking yellow flames painted on his skin from his waist to his shoulders, a dyed-scarlet feather in his topknot, a bow in his left hand and an arrow nocked for business. He ran with his face down, eagle-sharp eyes picking out Matt's prints.

Because of his elevated position, Matt sighted on the area just above the brave's driving left-right, left-right knees, and squeezed the trigger. The butt slapped his shoulder and the pan and muzzle spewed smoke and through the swirl he saw the Abenaki run right into the ball and double over it, still coming on, his legs chopping in the empty air as his head and the crimson feather whipped down with a streak

142

of vivid color and struck the ground, and his body following in a quick flattening somersault.

The second Abenaki, twenty yards behind, leaped to one side of the path and into cover, letting out a *Yu-Yu!* And the third sprang to the other side and disappeared. Matt couldn't see the rest.

He turned and crawled out of the rocks and went down the back of the slope in a humped run, heading for the woods. It was a variation of the old fox trick and he simply loved it.

They had seen him barricade himself in a natural fortress. They had seen him prepare to defend his position. Now they would lose valuable time sending braves right and left to flank the position. If he was lucky he might gain as much as ten minutes before they discovered he had tricked them and was long gone.

He heard the *pak-pak* of their muskets as they chipped away at the empty little rock fort. He ran grinning. But he wasn't lucky . . . not ten minutes' worth.

"*Hee-yaa!*" an enraged shriek rang out.

He crossed a shallow stream, pausing only to cast the musket upstream. Maybe he'd return for it some day: probably not. Anyhow it wasn't any good to him now, and it was a relief to get rid of the twelve extra pounds.

He dug into the grubsack as he ran and popped corn into his mouth. When he forded the next creek he scooped up water with his hands and drank it on the run.

He was going good now. He had his second wind. He breathed deeply through his mouth, keeping his head high and his knees low. His crooked arms worked at his sides like pistons, back-forth, back-forth.

He felt that he could run all day. And he would probably have to.

When he looked back he saw one Abenaki far far in the lead of his brothers. He was stripped bare, down to feather,

143

war paint, moccasins and tomahawk, and he was coming like a barrel down a steep hill.

This was the pacesetter. It wasn't his intention to catch Matt, merely to scare him into running faster, faster, until he winded himself to a frazzle. Then, in about half an hour, the first pacer would fall back to loaf along at a more normal lope, as the second pacer came forward and took over the job. They could keep this up for days if they had to and they could run down a deer, if given time.

Matt didn't let the pacesetter panic him; he let him think he had. He increased his speed and slowly pulled farther ahead, putting more and more ground between them. He had a good lead and he was going to need it. He had to have time to work a little trap.

Now he was in a stretch of bogland, leaving dandy tracks in his wake, and he plowed into a tall, vast bed of marsh grass fronting a timber brake. A cross-eyed Dutchman could follow his trail without even looking at the ground, and that was just what he wanted.

As the tall grass ended a sapling thicket picked up. He selected a man-high sapling, tested it for spring, and stepped off the path to go to work.

He cut a small forked branch with one tine shorter than the other, cocked the sapling back to the ground, lashed his knife to it with a bit of thimblevine, aiming the blade down-trail, secured the sapling with the fork, tied another length of vine to the fork, payed out the vine for a few feet, took a turn with it around another sapling, then brought it at a right angle onto and across the path and tied it to a root.

The trigger vine was about two inches above the leaf-matted path. He covered it with a windrow of soggy leaves, as though a low-scudding wind had ridged the leafy carpet. Then he stepped over the trigger and laid some heavy-footed tracks into the thicket.

If he could find enough water, and if he could gain

enough time, he could lay some false tracks and then escape up or down a stream.

Suddenly a spine-clutching shriek reached for a high note but didn't make it. By grab, he thought. I got him!

Then, through the screen of tules and saw-blade grass, he saw a fat, merry stream running north. He started upstream, his feet in the water. Within an hour he reached the Conemaugh. He thought he was safe. For a while, maybe.

Dusk was just beginning to concern itself with evening when Matt came trotting into the quiet Seneca village east of Laurel Ridge. Right away the Indian dogs knew about him and they came bowling out of the nearly empty lodges all furious barks and bared teeth. Matt threw rocks at them with unerring aim and they took off with their tails between their legs, *ky-ying* to beat the band.

Cautiously the children and old men and women came to their hide-hung doors and looked at him. Some of the boys and old men fingered their hatchets undecisively. Matt helped them make up their minds.

There was a drum in the communal clearing made of a tree trunk as big around as an overland wagon wheel. He sprang up to it and raised an arm to the expectantly waiting lodges.

"He'onwe hadi'nonge ne Otgon?" he called. "Where is the dread power of evil magic? *I'iet Otgon!* He stands next to you. I am he! I am He-Who-Climbs-to-*ne Hanisheonon-'ge!*"

They had heard the tale all right. He saw the fear sparkle in their obsidian eyes. Some of them even shrank back involuntarily. If this strange white man could climb to the Evil One's cave and laugh in the Evil One's face, what could he not do to poor Seneca children and old men and women? It was too horrible to contemplate.

"He'onwe hadi'nonge ne Haksa'dase'a Ni'haia'do'den?"

145

Matt demanded furiously. "Where is the white captive? Bring him forth!"

They hesitated. They averted their eyes. One old duffer opened his mouth tentatively to speak. Matt didn't give him the chance. He swept his raised arm down to the horizontal and pointed at them.

"Quick! Or I will turn you all to *ne henes ne ge'gach'ys!*"

None of them wanted to be turned into vile, long-tailed lizards. The women moaned tragically, the children cowered out of sight, and a few old men went tottering off to the council house in a hysteria of haste. Matt tapped his foot on the drumhead impatiently. The gesture wasn't all for show. He had no idea how far behind were the Abenakis. They were probably throwing ring hunts along the fork of the Conemaugh.

Two of the old men were leading a ragged youth between them. The boy's wrists were lashed and they had kept him hobbled with rawhide.

That's bad, Matt thought. He won't be worth a hoot when it comes to running. "Cut him loose!" he commanded.

They hastened to do his bidding and the boy started rubbing his sore wrists and stomping his numb legs. He couldn't have been more than sixteen, and looked as if he'd been scared for a long long time.

"Have you come to get me out a here, mister?"

"Yes. And quick! Let's get up on the ridge. What's your name?"

"Tyke Hall—and I guess it would a been Angel Hall if it wasn't for you!"

I wish we had the wings of angels, Matt thought grimly. We could sure use 'em! They took off for the woods.

They didn't get far; Hall's legs just didn't have it in them. They rested in the scrub alongside the ridge as dusk began to steal toward them like a cat-footed thief, and they talked.

"Why did you desert, Hall?" Matt wondered.

"Mister, you would've too. It took us five days to get from Wills Creek to Great Meadows, and ever' day Mr. Curry would grow more worried than the day afore. He'd keep sayin' things like: 'Hope it ain't true Washington's gonna leave us out here for the French'n Injuns.' And when we'd ask him what he meant, he'd say he'd heard a rumor that we was only a decoy for the enemy."

Matt gawked at the boy. "Harry?" he said blankly. "Harry Curry said those things to you?"

Hall nodded his head vigorously. "Bet your boots he did. And more, much more. We got so jumpy by the time we reached Great Meadows we nearly shot a friendly half-breed we met there."

Harry Curry had deliberately spooked the advance supply party! Matt couldn't believe it. He grabbed Tyke Hall's arm. "What's this about a friendly half-breed?"

"That's right. We'd just made our camp when this breed came pokin' in on his horse. We nearly shot him dead we was so rattled! But he told us he wasn't all Injun, and he seemed to recognize Mr. Curry."

"Listen," Matt said urgently. "Was it Cassanna?"

"Cassanna? I don't know no Cassanna. And I didn't know this man; but Mr. Curry did, I guess. They went off a ways and had a parley. I couldn't hear 'em, but I was watching 'em. Mr. Curry pointed off toward the Forks, and this breed took the feather out a his topknot and then got a beaver cap from his saddlebag. And you know, when he pulled it over his head he looked just like a white man. Because he was wearing boots and pants and a deerskin shirt, and he had blue eyes."

Matt didn't know what to think. It didn't make sense. Harry Curry was the traitor who had deviously tried to frighten Washington's army into turning back! But why? For godsake why?

Hall was tugging desperately at Matt's sleeve.

147

"Mister—Mister, there he is now!"

Matt came out of his daze with a start, his head jerking up.

"What? Who?"

Hall was pointing toward a pawpaw not ten yards away. A man stood there in the gathering gloom. He was watching them and he held a musket in his hands and he wore boots, pants, a deerskin shirt, and a feather in his topknot.

"I had an idea it was you we were chasing, Burnett," Cassanna said. "But we never came close enough to you to tell. You're pretty good for a white man on the run. If it hadn't been for your friend there, you'd have made it."

"Yes," Matt said, rising slowly to his feet, looking around. A segment of the ring hunt had caught up to them . . . how far away were the others? Cassanna, coming closer, seemed to read his thought.

"Some more Abenakis will be along shortly," he said. He looked at Tyke Hall. "I've seen this boy before."

"At Great Meadows," Matt told him. "Where Harry Curry secretly turned-coat and joined you. Why did he do it, Cass? His father—"

Cassanna showed his French blood by shrugging. "His mother was French—just as mine was. Perhaps he wants vengeance on the colonists who killed her at Louisburg. Perhaps the part of him that is French believes as I do, that this land belongs to the French and Indians; and we mean to take it, now!"

Matt moved a step, another one, toward Cassanna.

"You're wasting your time, Cass. It can't be done. You don't know the men you're up against . . . and neither does Harry."

Cassanna laughed scornfully. "Poor fool, you don't know the odds that're coming against your pitiful excuse for an army. Coulon de Villiers, the brother of Jumonville, is now preparing to march from Fort Duquesne with six hundred

148

Frenchmen and four hundred Indians! Yes, nine nations have contributed to the effort: Hurons, Abenakis, Mingoes, Nipissings, Algonquins, Ottawas, Miamis, Sacs, and even the Delawares. They will sweep over Washington like a red tide!"

It was a grim bit of news, and Matt didn't doubt its veracity. Cassanna, thinking that Matt and Hall would shortly be dead, had no reason to lie. Matt took another step, and Cassanna leveled the musket at his hip.

"Stop right there, Burnett."

Matt stopped. He thought, If we don't do something we're both dead men. Maybe one of us can still get away.

He removed the tomahawk from his belt and passed it to Hall.

"The moment he shoots me—jump him and kill him with this."

He started forward again, slowly. Cassanna went back a step.

"Don't be a fool, Burnett! I'll shoot you like a dog."

"I guess you'll have to," Matt told him. "If you don't, I'll kill you with my bare hands. C'mon," he said to Hall.

It put Cassanna in a touchy spot. He only had one shot; if he killed Matt, Hall would get him with the hatchet. If he killed Hall, Matt would charge with his knife. He deliberated, then said, "Wait."

He disarmed the musket by removing the flint. Then he leaned the gun against the pawpaw. He drew his own tomahawk, saying, "Return Burnett's hatchet," to Hall.

Matt nodded to Hall and took back his tomahawk. He could feel his stomach shriveling with tension. Then, Cassanna going into a sudden crouch and Matt doing the same, he forgot about his stomach, about everything. He concentrated wholly on the fight.

Cassanna came with a rush, yelping, *"Eee-yu!"* And swerved to the right just as Matt put up his guard, and then

149

slowed and started to circle. Matt turned with him, moving on a small tight pivot.

Cassanna rushed again, his tomahawk flashing up, Matt swinging his into position; and again the breed stopped short and all at once and started to circle in the opposite direction. Matt turned slowly.

"Eee-yu!" Cassanna came the third time. Matt crouched, his left hand touching ground, scooped up some damp dirt and threw it at the breed's contorted face, leaping left as Cassanna blundered confusedly to a halt and started hatchet-swinging blindly.

Matt sprang forward, aiming a telling blow. But the handful of tossed dirt had been too moist to be effective. It had distracted Cassanna momentarily, it hadn't actually blinded him. He stepped adroitly outside the arc of the blow and countered with a horizontal sweep at the side of Matt's head.

Matt ducked under it and side-stepped to the left and straightened up just in time to cry a warning to Tyke Hall.

"Look out!"

Cassanna, finding himself within four paces of Hall, had decided to dispatch the enemy spectator with one quick chop, and he would have succeeded if it hadn't been for Matt's shout.

Hall stumbled clear in a frantic backing run, and Cassanna had to forget him and swing his attention around to Matt who was charging fast and silent. Then Matt yelled, "Yah!" and slammed to a stop and crouched off to the right, circling Cassanna this time.

Cassanna panned with him, watching him warily, like a coiled rattler. He decided to try a little psychology on Matt. He sneered and started to taunt him.

"How old were you when I taught you to fight with a tomahawk, twelve? I believe you were better at it then than you are now. And even then I beat you every time!"

That was the truth, Matt recalled. But he pretended that

150

it didn't bother him. "You were fourteen or more, then," he reminded Cassanna. "That's a big difference between children. But it doesn't mean a hoot now that we're men."

Abruptly Cassanna took off from a full stop, charging straight into Matt, the tomahawk raised over his shoulder and already starting on the downswing. It was so sudden it was totally distracting, and for a vivid instant Matt's equilibrium went out of whack and all he could do was react automatically, ducking, swinging his hatchet on an up-oblique, but without timing; his sweep missed Cassanna's chest by six inches and if his body hadn't followed through with the blow, lunging to the right, his skull would have been parted. As it was Cassanna's tomahawk cleaved off the deerskin thumbs on his left shoulder.

He felt the sting of the blow on his arm as he got out of there in a near panic. Then he stopped, got himself back in hand, and crouched into position again. They were fifteen feet apart.

Cassanna smiled thinly and glanced at the ground. He went one to two steps left and started to crouch down, his left hand reaching for something on the ground as he watched Matt.

Matt shot a quick look toward the searching brown hand. A long stick was in the weeds and if Cassanna got it he would use it to ram between Matt's legs and trip him up. But the gesture was a deliberate trick to distract Matt's attention. Cassanna never meant to use the stick.

The instant Matt's eyes flicked toward the reaching hand, Cassanna cocked his tomahawk over his shoulder and fired it haft-over-head.

"Duck!" Hall screamed.

But he didn't have to; Matt had already sent himself into a headlong body dive to the right.

He heard the *wwwhup* of the spinning hatchet hum over his hip and right then his body slammed the ground full-

151

length, and he rolled on his left side, cocking his tomahawk arm back as Cassanna came at him like a springing panther, the whites of his eyes brilliant in his darkly grimaced face, the feather over his head bending in the momentum of his rush, and the scalping knife now in his raised right hand.

Matt let his tomahawk fly and there wasn't more than four feet of air between them when he did, and Cassanna was already tilting into a deadly knife-plunge and there was no stopping his body even after the tomahawk went *thok* in his chest. He kept right on coming, barreling over Matt's prone body, and that was the way he ended up—his legs covering Matt's waist. He didn't move.

The exuberant Hall helped Matt to his feet. Matt was trembling badly and, now that it was over, his stomach was going crazy again. Also Hall was pounding him on the back, which was annoying.

"Man alive, did you nail him! And just when I thought he had you cold!" He looked at the dead half-breed angrily, saying, "Dirty dog! Him and his kind would a burned me at the stake! The dirty—"

"Shut up," Matt said shortly, remembering Cassanna now as a youth, recalling some of his words from way back when . . . *No, no. Don't throw a tomahawk that way. You'll never hit anything. Do it the way I show you . . .*

"Well, he was a murderin' Abenaki savage, wasn't he?" Hall insisted.

But Matt shook his head. "No. He was a confused man, caught between two races. He thought he was right."

And maybe, Matt reflected, that was the real tragedy in war: both sides were certain that they were right.

"Let's go," he said quietly.

13

THE TURNCOAT

It was the second night after the evening of Cassanna's death. It was the twenty-eighth of June and Matt and Tyke Hall were stumbling through the last belt of woods facing Great Meadows. They were dead on their feet; worse, so Hall mumbled, he had no feet left. He was ambulating on numb stumps; he had walked his feet off up to the ankles. Matt had nothing to say. He saved his wind for his body.

Then Hall blundered into some dead branches on the ground and they crackled under his feet as though they were being consumed by fire. Instantly a shout rang out from somewhere up ahead, and immediately afterward a musket blared in the dark.

"Hi!" Matt hailed. "Fort Necessity, hold your fire! We're Americans. I'm Matt Burnett from Captain Hoag's company!"

It was the Carolina sentries who ushered them into camp. They were nervous and trigger-itchy and treated Matt and

Hall like prisoners of war. They herded them toward the stockade at bayonet point.

The meadow seemed strangely empty of Virginians and Indians. Men kept gathering around them in the glaring light of torches, staring at them with open expressions of suspicious anger, like a band of sullen brothers. All of them, as far as Matt could see, were regulars.

"Where's Washington?" he demanded. "I have information for him."

One of the regulars snorted a laugh. "Bet you do, if you're Burnett!" he said enigmatically.

Matt didn't like the feeling of distrust and anger that emanated from the regulars. He decided to keep his mouth shut until he reached his own people. The regulars led them into the stockade and over to Washington's command tent. A light was glowing merrily through the slope-walled canvas.

A regular went to the flap, raised it, and spoke to someone inside.

"Sir, we've got a couple of deserters back."

A gruff voice answered something, and the soldier motioned Matt and Hall forward, saying, "The CO will see you now."

There was only one man inside the tent. He was sitting on a keg behind the hardtack-box desk; a candle guttered in the butt-end of a bayonet which had been driven point-first into the top of the box, and the quivering flame tossed a wavy orange light over his bland face.

Captain Mackay was the commanding officer of Fort Necessity.

Mackay looked at Matt, at Hall, back to Matt again. He said, "You must be a fool, Burnett, to simply walk in and give yourself up. It would be one thing if you belonged to the Virginia militia; but you don't. You're a volunteer, and

154

volunteers are subject to Crown army regulations . . . to court-martial and firing squad for desertion."

"Captain, I don't know what you're talking about," Matt told him. "I'm not a deserter. But there's no time for that now; I've got to see Colonel Washington. I have information for him."

"Do you?" Mackay's blunt tone implied that he doubted it. "Well, you're out of luck. Washington and his Virginians have decamped."

"Gone? But why? Where?"

Captain Mackay looked peevishly unhappy. "Because he's the spoiled pet of that old fool Dinwiddie. Because he wants everything his way. Told me that the situation in this camp was intolerable; that my men were demoralizing his men; and he had the gall to say this to me:

" 'You want this camp for nothing. Very well, take it. I'm going to advance to the Redstone and set up a base to combat the enemy.' "

Matt digested the information and realized that it was the kind of action that Washington with his firebrand impulsiveness would take. If the French wouldn't come to him, he would go to them.

But it meant that he was proceeding with only two hundred and fifty men, not knowing that his Indian allies had deserted him, or that a force of one thousand was preparing to advance against him.

"Captain, I've got to see Colonel Washington. It's imperative. There must be some way we can contact him."

Mackay gave a dour nod. "I understand he's only gone as far as Gist's cabin. But I doubt if he'll be very happy to see you. After all, you and that Holly were under suspicion before you deserted."

"We didn't desert, captain. We went to the You River for information. All the local Indians were going to hold a

155

powwow to decide whether or not to fight for Washington."

Mackay began to show a little interest. "So?"

"So the decision is no. They are going to remain neutral . . . except the Delawares. We learned later that they will fight for the French."

Mackay wouldn't accept it. "You're lying!"

"Captain, where are the Seneca now? Where is Half King?"

"Why . . . why, they've gone out to invite the western and Ohio tribes to join us, to fight for us. Why, damme, man, Dinwiddie himself wrote that one thousand Cherokee and Catawba would be coming to our aid; and the Shawnees . . ." His voice petered out. Matt was shaking his head.

"No sir, you're deceiving yourself. Half King has walked out on us, and the others simply aren't coming. But I'll tell you what is coming—six hundred Frenchmen and four hundred Indians from nine tribes. Hall and I received this information from Cassanna, and Cassanna was a big sachem in the Abenaki nation."

Mackay glared distractedly at Hall. "And who is this Hall —this bedraggled-looking boy?"

"He's a Virginia militiaman, and he's been a Laurel Ridge captive for two months. He has information regarding a traitor in our army."

But Mackay wasn't actually listening. He had something more important to worry about than a traitor. There he was in command of a crackerbox fort with no artillery and only one hundred fair-weather soldiers, and here was this youth leaning over his desk telling him that he might expect to be attacked by one thousand French and Indians at any hour. One thousand!

"If you're lying, Burnett . . ." His voice was a bare whisper.

Matt could see that he had already reached the King's officer.

156

"It's the truth, sir. Your order to consolidate all our forces at Gist's might save the day." He thought that was diplomatically put. Evidently Mackay did too; it looked as though the order to march had been his idea. He left his seat with alacrity.

"Orderly! Order the drums rolled. We march at once!"

Hall had reached the dropping point and Matt wasn't far from it. Mackay had them mounted on horses, and even so two mounted regulars had to be assigned to ride on either side of Hall to secure him against falling to sleep in the saddle and toppling to the ground.

Mackay, Matt and Hall, and a handful of men rode on ahead of the regulars. Now that Mackay had been apprised of the true situation, and his fears of annihilation had been ignited, the soldier side of his nature came to the fore and he had become all business. No time was to be wasted in reaching Washington. The horses were not spared.

It was the dark before the dawn when Mackay's party reached Gist's little settlement. All around them they could see the start of a temporary fortification; but it was not much—an entrenchment backed by some fencing, somewhat in the form of a palisade.

Lieutenant Murcer was officer of the guard and he led them to Gist's cabin. Matt held back before entering, to speak to Mackay in a low tone.

"One favor, captain," he requested. "Keep Hall out here with your men until I ask for him. Keep him out of sight."

Mackay didn't understand it but he was grudgingly agreeable. Oddly enough, this young man (whom he had been prepared to shoot for desertion a few hours before) had slowly gained the glowing aspect of a valuable soldier in his harassed mind.

Candles and slush lamps spluttered and flared inside the cabin, and Matt watched the slow gathering of the sleep-stupid officers. Washington sat behind a hand-hewn board

157

table, yawning and rubbing at his face. He was in his pants and shirt, no boots. He looked at Matt critically but reserved comment.

Major Muse, Captains Hoag, Lewis, Vanbraam, Stephen, and Stobo, Ensigns Ward and Peyroney were all there. And so was Harry Curry, in a blue uniform jacket. Harry had been made an ensign.

"Colonel," Mackay started right in, "we've been sold out. Burnett here and his friend Holly have been to an Indian powwow, and their information is that not one of our Indian allies will back us in a fight against the French. This includes Half King, colonel."

Washington removed his level gaze from Mackay and set it on Matt.

"Let's take first things first. Burnett, are you aware that you and Holly have been posted as deserters?"

"Yes, sir. But we did not desert. Shad Holly heard from his Seneca friend Chief of the powwow, which would determine the status of the local Indians in the event of a shooting war. We decided we should sit in on it and find out their decision."

"So you slunk out of camp without permission or notification."

"Yes, sir. There was no other way. We knew we were already under suspicion for something we weren't guilty of. Suppose we'd come to you or any of these officers . . . would you have let us go?"

Washington's mouth twitched, perhaps in wry amusement. There was something in what Matt said; to begin with he had never even trusted Chief. He wondered now if this had been a mistake.

"And yet," he said, "it would seem that by your action you have proven nothing. You are still under suspicion; more so now than ever."

"But not for long, sir," Matt replied. "I've found out who

158

the traitor is: the person who deliberately spread every vicious and frightening rumor he could dream up to hamstring this army."

He looked at Harry, who stared back with unperturbed indifference.

Matt turned to Mackay. "Captain, when you first joined us at Fort Necessity you immediately began to hear these various disturbing rumors, didn't you? Can you tell us whether the rumors filtered up to you through your men, or did they start directly through one of the colonel's men?"

Mackay gave it some thought. Suddenly his look brightened.

"Why, I believe it was Ensign Curry who first told me some of the things that were being said."

Matt had thought so. He had noticed right from the beginning that Harry and Mackay had become very chummy, but he hadn't attached any meaning to it at the time.

All the officers turned to Harry. He looked back at them levelly.

"Mr. Curry, is this true?" Washington asked.

"All I did was repeat what I had already heard from others," Harry said calmly.

"Oh? Surely that wasn't very wise of you, was it?"

"If I was in error, I apologize," Harry said stiffly. "But I was concerned over the management of this expedition. I thought Captain Mackay, as a King's officer, should understand the situation."

"He did more than repeat the rumors, sir," Matt said. "He created them." He looked at Harry again. "You deliberately scared the men in your advance party into deserting, by telling them over and over that the colonel was only using them as a decoy to lure the French. And through your act our advance supplies were lost.

"You ran into Cassanna, whom you knew as a boy, at Great Meadows and told him you wanted to help the

159

French defeat the Virginians. You sent him to the Forks to tell Tram and Ward the same lies you had been telling your own men."

Harry made a sound of contempt in his nose. "Can you prove any of this? Of course not! You're merely trying to get yourself out of trouble by foisting the blame onto me."

"Did you know Cassanna as a boy?" Washington asked.

"Slightly. He and his father stayed at Burnett's home for a fortnight."

"Did you see him at Great Meadows?"

"I did not."

"Did you send a rider, anybody, to the Forks to see Tram and Ward?"

"I did not."

Washington turned to Ward. "You don't know who the rider from Great Meadows was? Was he an Indian?"

Ward looked baffled. "I didn't know him, sir. I thought he was a white man—blue eyes, dark skin, dressed like a backwoodsman . . ."

"It was Cassanna," Matt insisted. "And Curry sent him. I talked to Cassanna three days ago by the Laurel Ridge village."

Harry's look was pure scorn. "So you say. Prove it."

"I couldn't by Cassanna—I killed him."

There was a stir among the officers and an audible murmur.

"Oh yes," Harry sneered. "It's easy to say you killed him, and make yourself out to be quite the hero. But you know very well that you can't prove it."

Washington pursed his lips and looked at Matt.

"Did you kill Cassanna?"

"Yes, sir. I had to. His Abenakis were after me."

"But can you prove it?"

"Yes, sir. I had a witness."

"How much of this nonsense must we listen to?" Harry

160

snapped. "I suppose you'll tell us next that your witness was Shad Holly. And every man here knows that Holly is the biggest liar in Pennsylvania. And they also know that he'd say black was white if you asked him to!"

Matt smiled at Harry. "Shad wasn't my witness. Shad and Chief were over on the You River detaining the Laurel Ridgers from returning to their village, where I was collecting the witness."

"Come, come, Burnett," Captain Hoag said impatiently. "Who was the witness?"

Matt turned to Mackay. "Sir, will you order that boy in here?"

All of the officers stared at the doorway as Mackay put his head out and snapped an order into the darkness. Matt glanced at Harry. The new ensign had a narrowing look around his arrogant eyes and his eyes didn't blink as he watched the door.

There was a stir and a clump of weary boots, and then the bedraggled, half-asleep Hall stood there in the doorway batting his red-rimmed eyes against the light. He looked at the officers slowly, one at a time, until he came to Harry. He straightened up involuntarily, and slow anger began to kindle in his tired eyes.

"Mr. Curry, you shouldn't have told us all them lies. You almost got me Injun-kilt!"

14

PRO PATRIA!

It must have been an unnerving moment for Harry. But if the shocking sight of Hall disconcerted him, he recovered rapidly. His hand went inside his jacket and whipped out a pistol, which he promptly clapped to the side of Washington's head.

"No one move," he ordered crisply. "Get up and walk me over to the door," he told Washington.

The young commander paused as though in thought. Then he shook his head. "No. I won't help you, in any way. You should know by now that coercion has little effect on me."

Harry hesitated and ran his eyes around the ring of immobile faces watching him. He turned the pistol on Matt. "If anyone attempts to hinder my departure, I'll shoot the Pennsylvania hero."

"There is no need for these melodramatics, Mr. Curry," Washington said coldly. "You may put up your weapon and walk out of here unharmed. You see, we are done with you."

For the first time since Matt had known him Harry appeared uncertain. It seemed to be Washington's cold words "we are done with you" that did it. There was something so prophetically final about them.

Harry stalled a moment longer, then started for the door. But he kept the pistol trained on Matt all the way. No one said anything, did anything. Mutely they watched him go. Then, as the door slammed after him, there was an angry uproar, which Washington stilled by raising his hand.

"Let him go. He is no longer important. He's made his bed, now we'll see how he likes it." He turned his attention back to Matt.

"I owe you and your friend Holly my most profound apologies. I confess that in moments of great harassment I found myself doubting your loyalty. Will you allow me the opportunity of making small amends by appointing you an ensign's commission?"

Matt grinned. "Thank you, sir, but I think I'll turn it down. You see, I'm afraid it might hurt Shad's feelings; he always likes to think of himself as the leader of the First Pennsylvanians."

Washington laughed. "Then I fear we'll have to give Holly a lieutenancy in order to make you an ensign."

After that the static atmosphere in the small cabin simmered down. Ward and Stobo came over to shake Matt's hand, while Mackay presented the appalling information that Matt had given him earlier.

"Gentlemen," Washington said, when Mackay had concluded, "our situation is, to say the least, dire. This position here, because of the surrounding hills, is untenable. Fort Necessity, for the same reason, isn't much better; but certainly more advantageous for defensive combat than this. So, I propose to fall back en masse to Great Meadows.

163

"Our three most serious considerations are: lack of transport, food and ammunition. This then is the prospect: our soldiers must draw the swivels, they must content themselves on starvation rations, and when it comes to fighting they must make every shot count."

He stood up and looked at his grim-faced officers.

"If it is humanly possible," he said quietly, "let this retreat end at Great Meadows, and let us hold the country west of the Alleghenies and Laurel Ridge. It is a large order, I know; too large to even be put in the form of an order. I simply ask you to do your best. Dismiss!"

It was a slow hard march back to Fort Necessity. It cost the little army the better part of two days. The balky swivel guns were the biggest problem; the men sweated and swore and strained over them every foot of the way. There were only two wagons, clearly not enough to suffice even for the ammunition. Washington had to order his own riding horse to be loaded with powder and shot and, having set the example, his officers quickly followed suit. Personal baggage had to be abandoned.

The road, all rocks and stumps and grades, was the roughest and most hilly of any on the Allegheny Mountains, and Mackay's regulars refused to lend the Virginians a hand. It was ironic, for Mackay suddenly found himself in the same position as Dr. Frankenstein. When he had first arrived at Great Meadows he had created a monster in order to gain his own ends. Now, when he needed the monster, it turned on him. His men still refused to do a lick of work. They were soldiers of the King, they said. They were paid to fight, not to build roads and shove wagons. They would only work if they received an increase in pay, in advance.

Matt was glad that Shad was absent; otherwise he would have been brawling from one fistfight to another all the way up to a court-martial. Matt only hoped that when it came to combat the haughty regulars would condescend to load a musket and pull a trigger.

The half-starved, beat-to-the-knees army straggled into Great Meadows on the first of July. There was to be no rest for the weary. Washington was everywhere giving orders for the defense. A longer field of fire had to be cleared, the stockade had to be finished, the earth entrenchments enlarged, the command tent pulled down and a small shack thrown together inside the palisade, to house the powder and what few provisions the army had remaining.

The site of the frail fort had been poorly chosen. It was in a damp bottom in a narrow part of the meadow, commanded by three points of woods, with high ground hedging it in. The wooded slopes seemed to be grinning right into the heart of the little fort.

The Virginians were beginning to call Fort Necessity "Washington's rabbit trap."

"You can't tell me Harry didn't know what he was doing," Stefen told Matt angrily. "He picked this hole deliberately when he scared his men into deserting, knowing that Washington would have to come here to find the supplies, and figuring that by then it would be too late for the army to move on to better ground. He dumped us right into a natural trap!"

"Yes," Matt said soberly, "I'm afraid he did."

And there hadn't been much Washington could do about it either, he reflected. The advance supplies had been stolen by hostile Indians, Fry and his three companies had been far behind and, hamstrung by lack of supplies, men, and transport, Washington had been forced to camp where he was. And right after that the Jumonville incident had exploded; and that had been followed by the constant warnings of an immediate French attack.

"I don't know how the colonel's managed to hold on as long as he has, Steve," Matt said admiringly. "A lesser man

165

would have thrown up his hands in despair long ago and said to heck with it all."

"Yeah," Stefen agreed, reaching for his spade, "he's stubborn. He makes up his mind to do a thing and you can't dislodge him with a crowbar."

Stubborn—yes, that was one word for it, Matt supposed. But loyal, he felt, was a word much closer to the mark.

And that night when he crawled into his damp little lean-to he picked up Tammy's claymore and cradled it in his lap and seemed to derive a measure of courage and strength from it.

To all the soldiers, everywhere, from any time or age, he thought reverently, who fought and bled and died for the cause they believed in—I am brother to you tonight. Tammy, whatever comes tomorrow, we'll face it together. You will go with me, be with me through this sword.

Then he curled up in his blanket, the old claymore that had lost a kingdom at Culloden Moor in his right hand, and dropped into deep dreamless sleep. The next day was the third of July.

The *pak* of a musket greeted the steely dawn. From the woods came a shout for the sergeant of the guard. The Americans tumbled groggily from their blankets, snatching up muskets, powder horns, shot bags, everyone asking his sleep-dazed neighbor, "What is it? Who fired? What's happening, for grab's sake?"

Rapidly the word was passed back that someone had fired on one of the sentries. The man had suffered a wound in the heel. No, he didn't know who had shot him; it was still too dark in the woods to see.

"Places! Places!" the officers were shouting. "Get to your posts! Keep your powder dry! By nathun, you'll need it today!"

Matt shoved his tomahawk in his belt, strapped Tammy's

166

sword around his waist, and picked up his musket. Hurriedly he entered the enclosure of the entrenchments and made his way to the northwest salient. Captain Hoag caught sight of him and shouted:

"Get down to the end, Burnett! Peyroney's squad is holding that position!"

Matt trotted over to the end of the trench, where it stopped abruptly and pointed at the little ribbon of water in the gully, and tossed Peyroney a salute. Just then Lieutenant Murcer caught him by the elbow.

"Burnett, you're not authorized to wear a sword!"

Peyroney called from the trench. "Lieutenant, the officer you are manhandling is Ensign Burnett. That's by the colonel's order, sir."

"Sorry," Murcer mumbled, and gave Matt a slap on the back.

Matt jumped into the trench and grinned at Peyroney.

"Thought you had an objection to this sword?"

Peyroney shook his head seriously. "That was long ago when I didn't know any better. Let's get ready."

Half of the swivel guns had been mounted on the parapet between the stockade and the trenches; the other half had been placed inside the stockade with their narrow barrels poking between the palings of the palisade. Captain Stephen was in charge of the artillery, and he was concerned that his guns would be firing right over the heads of the men in the trenches. But nothing could be done about it. *C'est la guerre,* as the French would say. It is war.

Now, everyone nervously leaning over his gun, every pair of eyes fixed anxiously on the drab wall of the circling woods, they waited. Now the long apprehensive hours crawled by like a wounded snake. Nothing happened. Seven o'clock, eight, nine, ten . . . Nothing.

Except rain rain rain.

Then they heard the *plam* of a musket and a moment

167

later a burly man lumbered from the woods and started legging it across the clearing.

"Say, lookit that fat man travel!" a Virginian marveled. "He must have all of Canada shaggin' him!"

Matt climbed to the top of the earth embankment and yelled down the trenches. "Hold your fire! That's Shad Holly!"

Shad came hotfooting it through the wet weeds for all he was worth, spotted Matt on the north salient and swerved his course.

"Hi-yi, Matty!" he roared. "I see you still got your hair!"

He raised his hat and pointed to his own head, grinning. "Me too!"

Washington came from the stockade calling across the parapet.

"We all admire your noble head of hair, Lieutenant Holly. But would you mind giving us your report first?"

Shad, puffing and blowing for wind, stopped and blinked at him.

"Lieutenant Holly?" he echoed blankly. "Did you say Lootenant Holly, colonel?" Then the wonder of it dawned upon him and he snapped himself to attention and gave what he thought was a regulation salute, even though it looked as if he were trying to slap his right eye backhand, and said, "Yes sir, colonel! Lootenant Holly reporting!"

"Well, what is your report, man? Have you seen the enemy?"

"Have I seen the enemy?" Shad looked as if he'd come adrift from his wits. "That's all I been seein' for a week. Them woods is simply a-crawl with French'n Injuns! Me'n Chief have been following 'em all the way from the Forks, pickin' off the stragglers when there weren't nobody looking. Old Chief's still out there in the scrub adding to his scalp belt."

Yes, he told them, Villiers had at least six hundred soldiers and four hundred Indians. He was keeping one hun-

168

dred of the latter in the rear as a reserve, and it was these savages that Shad and Chief had been harassing on the sly.

Villiers' army had swept up the Monongahela in their canoes, reaching the mouth of Redstone Creek on the thirtieth, and had then started their march through the forest. On July second they reached the abandoned fortification at Gist's settlement and bivouacked in the pouring rain. At dawn the march was resumed. They passed through the gorge at Chestnut Ridge and made their way under the dripping forest to Jumonville's Glen, where an embittered Villiers held silent communion with his dead brother.

"Then you know what happened?" Shad cried peevishly. "That peewit Harry Curry came out a the brush and handed himself over to Villiers! Yes sir, I seen it myself! Started yammerin' French at 'em like a regular frog-eater. I couldn't make out what they was parleyin' about, but it appears that Harry offered to lead 'em straight to us! That's when I left Chief and come running on ahead."

"Quick, man," Washington snapped. "How close are they now?"

"How close are they?" Shad cried. "Is hangin' onto my coattails close enough, colonel? They're swingin' around right now to come at you from the southwest!"

Washington turned a step away, his head down, deliberating on the situation. It was bad, very bad. Through desertion and sickness he was missing one-fourth of his manpower. At best he could only put three hundred men in the field. He reached a decision and gave a sharp order to Major Muse.

"Major, order the men out. We'll form a line in the meadow, if you please!"

It was the eleventh hour.

You could hear the *dddddddrum-rum-rum-rummm* of the enemy's long roll now, and the *pak-pak-paking* of the Virginia sentries' muskets on the skirmish line. Abruptly the

169

sentries were falling back in a hysteria of hurry, shouting, "They're coming! They're coming!"

The Americans were in a long line across the meadow, facing the open ground on the southwest, the trenches and stockade right at their backs, the Union Jack whipping sluggishly on its post in the wet wind.

There was apprehensive grumbling. The Virginians and regulars didn't appreciate this stand-in-the-open method of combat. It made them feel like an army of empty-headed European toy soldiers waiting to be mown down. They glanced uneasily at their officers, who were glancing askance at Washington.

But the young colonel appeared to be undisturbed. He strolled in front of them, holding a sword in his hand, cutting at the weeds with it absently. Now and then he'd glance toward the southwest.

Like a mass escape from a madhouse the forest suddenly disgorged itself of howling Indians and shouting Frenchmen. They came pouring into the open with the drums tappity-tapping and the Mingoes wailing *eeeee-yuyuyu-yuuuu!* and the officers crying, *Attaque frontale, mes enfants!*

But the Mingoes and the Abenakis and the rest hadn't been brought up in the military schools of Europe and they didn't think a frontal attack in the open was worth a bag of beans . . . especially when two of Stephen's swivels cut loose with canister and bowled the front batch of painted savages over like rag dolls.

Quickly but not silently, hooting shrilly, the Indians deployed themselves to the right and left, seeking to encircle the little fort and its garrison under the shelter of the woods.

The French, distracted by this sudden reduction in their force, became rattled and opened fire at approximately six hundred yards. The Americans winced and ducked in place, Washington shouting, "Hold your line! Keep in order!"

They did, though they didn't like it. But they did.

170

"Shall we return their fire, sir?" Major Muse called.

Washington shook his head. "We'll wait for better targets." He turned to his men. "Don't let them intimidate you with mere noise."

Villiers wasn't quite certain what it was all about. When he'd first entered the meadow (even without his reserve) he had outnumbered the Americans three to one. Still the Americans had held their line. Then, as the Indians were chopped up by the swivels and had fanned out for cover, the odds in the field had dropped to two to one and the French had fired a volley which hadn't harmed the Americans in the least and to which they hadn't bothered to reply, and still they stood there in perfect alignment, waiting.

Villiers decided to press home his attack and run the stupid Americans into the earth with his bayonets. *"Attaque!"* he cried passionately. Charge! The French leveled their bayoneted muskets at the hip and pressed forward in a lumbering run over the field.

Then Washington triggered the trap.

"Fall back to the trenches! Prepare a volley!"

To the man the Virginians and regulars spun about and went leaping over the embankments into their trenches, bumping and banking into each other unheedingly and slipping, splashing in the mud and water, jostled elbows for firing room, leaning forward now behind the dirt parapet, leveled their guns down the field and sucked in their breath raspingly and seemed to freeze. And then the order, intoned, prolonged—a furious cry in the rain:

"FII—RE!"

The embankment blossomed an elongated mushroom of smoke and the meadow exploded with shot, and some of the raw troops must have been rattled and had forgotten to draw their ramrods, for a flight of rods sprang into the air like barbless, featherless arrows.

Matt saw the Frenchmen dropping, prostrating them-

171

selves frantically, then rising again before the Americans could reload and taking off across the meadow, every man for himself, some of them as close as sixty yards, with the Virginia muskets panning along on them and *plaming* after them.

An awkwardly running grenadier went past the north-west salient touching his smoldering match to a bulky-looking grenade in his hand as he ran, and then, the fuse spitting and hissing, halted, turned, and lobbed the grenade at the trench and took off again crouching low, as the iron ball came spinning through the air—everyone shouting *Look out!* and ducking behind the parapet.

The grenade bounced just outside of the embankment, and in the crash of gray smoke and orange flame a sheet of dark dirt sprang straight up and fell in a shower over the deafened Virginians.

The meadow was cleared. Matt could see the French and Indians in the woods now and along the scrubby hill slopes, running, ducking, dodging, firing; they were behind every little rise, every tree, stump, stone and bush. Their fire rained upon the embankments, the musket balls going *fut-fut-fut* in the dirt. From the hills they could rake a portion of the trench system and even a part of the interior of the stockade.

"The hills!" Stephen was shouting. "Train on the hills! Blow 'em out of there!"

The swivels swung around and the gunners elevated the barrels and touched them off, and all around the parapet they kicked back one after another going *KA-BLOWM! KA-BLOWM! KA-BLOWM!* right over the heads of the riflemen in the trenches, and the iron-banging crash felt as if your eardrums had been power-packed together regardless of your brains in between.

The hot shot went whining away gaudily and started punching holes in the wooded hills. Tops of trees went into

172

tilt and came crashing down, branches as big as rooftops pancaked everywhere, dirt fountains sprouted upward. The Indians hated the big guns. You could hear them yip-yipping about it furiously.

Robert Stobo came along the north trench in a crouch, squeezing behind the humped backs of the Virginia riflemen, French and Indian bullets *fut-fut-futting* in the dirt around him. He made it to Shad's burly side as a bullet kicked dirt in his face, and as he turned his head to wipe his eye another one spat dirt into his mouth and a third took a small chip out of his left earlobe. Feeling well peppered, he hunkered down in the trench mumbling Latin to himself.

"Timeo Danaos et dona ferentes; in short, 'Beware of the enemy who sends you presents.'" Then he looked up at Shad accusingly.

"Had I been born with wisdom I'd find myself a more tenable position in this accursed ditch. You're such a fat, inviting target you're drawing all their fire."

Shad beamed at his friend. "What're you kicking about?" he wanted to know. "I'm the target."

"True," Stobo agreed. "But unfortunately the marksmen appear to suffer from strabismus—cross-eyes, to you—for I'm receiving the brunt of the fire."

But he wasn't the only one. The enemy fire was becoming dangerously accurate. Virginians and regulars alike were throwing up their muskets, pitching over, slumping sideways, sprawling underfoot in the trenches, toppling on the cannon parapet. The wounded were quickly picked up and packed into the stockade.

Matt saw a Virginian four down from him suddenly bolt upright, saying *aaagh!* put his hands to his face and pitch backwards into the trench. It was an Ottawa who had made the hit and he'd fired from his hiding place in the little gully. Fantastically elated with his prowess as a marksman, he forgot the need for caution and sprang up from his place of

173

concealment with a triumphant war whoop. The Virginians applauded him with musket balls.

It rained water and shot. Then the liquid rain slacked off but the other did not. Then the Ottawas crept as close to the fort as they could, using stumps and stones and bush to great advantage, and added a new form of fire on the Americans.

Fire arrows.

The arrows skimmed sleekly through the air trailing fire and smoke, passing by with a *wwwunch* of murmuring wind, stabbing into the earth, into the stockade, worse—into the roof of the little supply house. The log-walled shack was covered over with bark and skins and some of the fire arrows penetrated the top layers of the roof and found dry substance to feed upon. Shortly the roof began to smolder, and men frantically tore it apart before a conflagration could gather and touch off the powder.

The fire arrows kept coming, describing brilliant parabolas across the sullen sky, falling, falling, *wwwunch-wwwunch-wwwunch,* the little bundles of grass lashed just behind the arrowheads bursting into dazzles of flame.

Then the sky opened up again and put an end to the fire arrows.

It rain rain rained. The fire slacked off on both sides. Men wiped at their faces, streaking themselves with grimy powder marks, looked around at each other, wet, shivering, hungry, miserable.

"For grab's sake, ain't nobody got nothin' to eat in this man's army?" a Virginian complained unhappily. "I sware my belly button's hung up on my backbone I'm so all-fired hongry!"

Matt dug in his grubsack and gave the man a portion of his Indian corn. "See if this'll unhook you," he offered.

The man tossed the corn into his capacious mouth without ceremony and talked around it as he chewed.

174

"You mind tellin' me what we're doin' out here in the middle of this blame wilderness, brother? With nuthin' but rain water to drink 'n musket balls to eat 'n French'n Injuns crawlin' down our backs by the hunnerds?"

Shad's indignant face loomed around Matt's shoulder. He said:

"I don't know about you, brother, but I'm here because my friends is here. And they're here because Washington is. And from what I understand he's here because he thinks this land belongs to me and my friends. That suit you?"

The Virginian chomped at his corn for a reflective minute, then his downcast features seemed to brighten a bit. "You know, that kind a makes sense, come to think on it."

"Yes, it sums it up rather nicely," Robert Stobo said, and he smiled fondly at Shad.

Fort Necessity was turning into a quagmire. The interior of the stockade was boot-top high with oozy mud, while the exterior gun rampart was a trampled slough. And the trenches were knee-high with water. Now when a man was hit, if he wasn't caught immediately by his friends, he'd submerge himself completely when he fell in the trench.

And then it got worse. The water inched higher. The sky was a vast overturned washtub. The rain became a deluge. It was all you could do to see the man standing next to you. The soldiers in the flooded trenches seemed to be floating. It was impossible to keep the rain out of your cartridge boxes; it soaked your charges and saturated your firelocks. It reached the powder that had been placed inside the shack.

Many of the Americans were now reduced to their bayonets, and some didn't even have that much to rely upon. Matt gave his bayonet to one of the Virginians, keeping his tomahawk and Tammy's sword for himself.

The rain took a breather and immediately the French fire opened up. The Americans were amazed that the enemy had managed to keep his powder dry. The return fire from the

175

fort was feeble, and this must have appeared as an encouraging sign to the Indians. They started whooping and yipping ecstatically, until the hills echoed with their cries.

Matt listened to the *Eeeee-yuyuyu-yuuuu* of the Mingoes and the *Keda-keda-kedmedaagik!* of the Abenakis and the *Coo-weegh-hh-hhh!* of the Ottawas and felt more than ever like a rabbit in a trap. The war cries ringed them in, going on around. They did something unpleasant to your stomach. They took the heart out of you. It was one thing to die by a musket ball in a fair fight. It was quite another thing to face Indian torture and the scalping knife.

The swivel guns were out of commission. It was worth a man's life to go near one, they were so exposed to French musketry; and besides, there wasn't enough dry powder left to waste on them.

Suddenly, through a gray veil of mist, a swarm of impetuous savages exploded into a pell-mell run toward the north trench. Paint-streaked, tomahawked, wild-haired with the Ojibway wolf tails and Ottawa horns and the deer-hair crests of Mingoes and fuzzy Abenaki scalp locks and the double dangling Huron feathers, they screeched like escaping demons out of some nether world pit.

Peyroney rose in the trench and pointed his sword at the leaping, bounding, howling swarm, shouting, "Fire!"

Matt's musket hung fire as the weak volley belched at the painted savages, and he threw it down and reached behind his back for his tomahawk as he watched Indians somersaulting, spinning, bouncing, sprawling into the weeds . . . but not enough of them. The red tide frothed vividly on, screaming gaudily.

"Bayonets! Out and at 'em! Forward!"

Matt and Shad stalled long enough to cock their tomahawks at their shoulders, then tossed them out together and the two foremost Ottawas went over backwards in a flashing blur of paint and horns and kicking beaded moccasins, and then they shoved up and over the muddy embankment with the thin line of Virginians, Shad with a musket clubbed by the barrel in his great square fists and Matt with Tammy's sword.

"At 'em! At 'em! Beat them bug-eaters back to Christmas!" Shad was beside himself. He threw his great body straight into the advancing savages and the musket butt simply flew right, left, right, left . . .

Matt dodged a tomahawk swing and hacked with the claymore and again and again. He felt totally numb in the chaotic howling confusion of winking bayonets, whipping feathers, flashing tomahawks, fists, knives, feet kicking, hands grabbing, voices voices . . . *Eeee-yuyu!* Look out! Behind you! Behind you! *Kedmedaagik!*

Men falling, running, muskets from the woods going *pak-pak,* muskets from the fort popping *plam! plam!* A hand on Matt's shoulder, a dragging weight—Peyroney, white-faced, wounded, saying, "Enough! We beat 'em. Get them back, Burnett."

Matt supported the wounded ensign in his arms, shouting for Shad.

"Shad! Take Peyroney! Fall back! Hoag's company—fall back to the trench!"

The weeds around his feet were a-hum with musket balls, going *thuk-thuk-thuk* in the mud. The savages were taking off along the gully in gaudy retreat, leaving one-third of their force behind. The Virginians were hurrying back to the trench grabbing up tomahawks for souvenirs as they ran. One thing you had to say for the American fighting man: he didn't give a dang how hot the fighting was as long as he got his souvenir, to remind him forever after just how rough it had been.

Matt piled back into the flooded trench and discovered that Shad had not only fetched in Peyroney but four tomahawks, an Ojibway wolf tail, and two Huron scalping knives

177

as well. He gave one tomahawk to Matt, and then went on down the line to see what he could swap the rest of his booty for. Matt could hear him splashing vociferously along.

"Brother, this ain't just any old Ojibway wolf tail. This here's a gen-u-wine sachem's headgear! I took it off him myself and I ort a know! What you got there? Four shillings? Lemme bite 'em first."

Matt bent over Peyroney. The wound was in his shoulder and he seemed to be in a mild case of shock.

"Burnett, is the flag still up?"

"Yes, sir. We beat 'em. The flag's all right."

"Show me."

So Matt helped him up and turned him and held him and pointed across the rampart to the Union Jack on its pole, the flag that Peyroney had raised himself five weeks before.

"It's a good flag," the ensign said softly. "It will suffice until we have a better one."

"Yes," Matt said. "You'll live to raise our own flag, some-day."

Peyroney nodded slowly. "I hope so, Matt. I hope I shall. I hope we'll all be there when it's done."

We will, Matt thought. One way or another—we'll be there.

15

THE AMERICANS

It was an unequal battle from the word go. The French definitely had all the advantage; and yet Villiers had problems of his own. After nine hours of fighting, Villiers, who had charged down from Fort Duquesne with blood in his eye, abruptly suffered an about-face of emotion and turned pacifist.

He was wet and he was cold; his soldiers were dead beat; his Indians had stopped whooping and were now grumbling about the rain and the lack of scalps and were threatening to decamp; he had seventy-three French casualties on his hands and he had no idea how many Indians had fallen; and now, to add to his mental and physical burden, excited aides kept running to him with the unwelcome news that they heard drums and cannon fire in the distance and that surely the English were executing a counterattack.

What they had heard had probably been thunder in the hills—yet how was Villiers to be certain? It was now eight o'clock, darkness had settled over the meadow, and the

179

battle had reached that appalling situation known in military circles as the stalemate.

Villiers dispatched an aide to the edge of the woods.

"Voulez-vous parler?" the aide called hopefully.

What in hades was that frog-eater jabbering about? the Americans wondered. Vanbraam translated the words to Washington and the young colonel shook his head.

"No, I won't parley. It's just a ruse of theirs to send an officer to our fort to see how we are situated." He and Vanbraam were hunkered on the lip of the trench just behind Matt's squad, and Matt saw Washington's teeth flash in the darkness of his face as he grinned.

"It isn't much fun to be flooded, to have no food or ammunition . . . but it would be a lot less fun if the French and Indians knew it. Tell them no," he ordered Vanbraam.

His officers were aghast.

"Man alive, this is our chance to get out!"

"We've had one hundred casualties—a third of our fighting force!"

"We must capitulate!"

Washington faced them angrily. "I know we must capitulate. But if we do it now it will be all their terms, and we won't have a say. Do you want to become prisoners of war? Or do you want the French to turn us loose unarmed in the woods for the Mingoes to scalp? Wake up, gentlemen! They wouldn't be making this overture if they weren't desperate. They don't seem to realize that they have us dead to rights."

"Non, s'il vous plaît!" Vanbraam shouted the decline.

There was a long pause, and then the French called again: Would the commander send out an officer who spoke French, to receive a proposal? Word of honor, the messenger would be permitted to return unharmed.

The stalling period was up. Washington nodded. "All right, Jacob. We've done our spadework, now let's see what results we can get. Tell them I will not capitulate without the condition that we retire from the fort with the full honors of war. You understand? A conditional capitulation is the only proposal I'll listen to."

He looked around in the dark. "An ensign should accompany Vanbraam."

Matt waded over to the lip of the trench. "May I go, sir?"

"Thank you, Mr. Burnett. Someone fetch them a torch."

Matt handed his musket to Shad and climbed from the trench with water draining noisily from his deerskins. Shad called after him.

"Matty, if you see Harry out there, tell him to enjoy himself with the French while he can. Because one a these days me'n Chief is gonna pay him a short little visit."

With a sputtering torch Matt and Vanbraam tramped off into the wet darkness, as the Virginians and regulars glumly retained their soggy posts in the flooded trenches.

A cadet greeted them with a snappy salute and ushered them into the woods and over to a group of officers standing about a lantern under the partial protection of a spreading tree. Villiers was very polite. He shook their hands; then he and Vanbraam got down to the business of drawing up a handwritten capitulation in French.

Matt stood back and looked around. Most of the French officers were regarding him with mute curiosity rather than animosity; but here and there the painted hawkface of an Indian glared at him with iron-eyed hate. He ignored them pointedly.

Then he spotted Harry Curry.

Harry didn't look at all like his usual natty self. He looked as tattered and bedraggled as Matt. There was a gaunt aspect about him which suggested that the French were also mighty low on provisions.

"Well, have you nothing to say to me?" Harry asked testily.

Matt had nothing to say to him. He simply looked at him.

181

Harry's eyes narrowed with barely controlled anger. "I only did what I thought was right! I had a debt to pay the provincials and I paid them in full coin. They killed my mother at Louisburg."

"That isn't true," Matt said. "I once heard your own father say that your mother died of a lung complaint. Just because the Americans had Louisburg bottled up at the time doesn't mean that they killed her. My father was there, and they didn't harm any civilians."

Harry brushed this truth aside unreasonably, childishly.

"All I'm concerned with is that she died there when your filthy rabble took the city away from the French!"

He was in fact being so unreasonable that Matt suddenly realized that Harry was trying to justify his traitorous action in Matt's eyes.

He's ashamed, Matt thought. He can't admit it, but he is.

"You're using that as an excuse. Why don't you admit the truth? You didn't sell out just to avenge your mother. And you didn't do it to help the French or to spite the English. You did it because you're a dyed-in-the-wool snob, because you hate the Americans, because you think you're so far superior to them."

Harry came closer, his eyes glassy and vicious in the lantern light.

"Yes," he hissed, "because I can see further than you, Burnett. I can see that your filthy backwoodsmen—the Americans, as you call them—are trying to take this land away from the aristocracy of Europe; as though they thought they had some claim to it!

"Your ignorant peasants have dreams of grandeur: they dream of setting themselves up as an independent nation! And if England doesn't have the foresight to see it and to stop them before it's too late, then I'm sure the French will. And I'll do everything in my power to help them keep this

182

land out of the grubby hands of your Shad Hollys and your Washingtons!"

Matt looked at the misguided youth and sensed a twinge of compassion for him. It wasn't the so-called ignorant backwoods Americans who lacked foresight, it was Harry. He was like Cassanna. He was living in the decadent past with the dying images of swords and roses and glittering knights and warlike land barons. To Harry, mankind was divided into two camps: the ruling class and the downtrodden peasants. And it simply wouldn't work in this new horizonless land. Harry was so shortsighted he was totally blind.

The capitulation paper was finished. Vanbraam nodded to Matt.

"Let's go, poy."

Matt looked at Harry and said, simply, "I trust you'll be very happy in Canada—with all your Abenaki aristocrats."

They walked away from the French, back across the misty meadow to Fort Necessity.

Washington gathered his officers together and they studied the capitulation paper under the guttering light of a candle, Vanbraam translating the written conditions for them.

Shad pulled Matt aside to ask, "You give that little peewit Curry my message?"

"No. To tell the truth, I don't have the heart to kick a man when he's down. And Shad . . . Harry's down, far down, and I think he knows it."

Vanbraam's limping translation took a long time and there was a great deal of haggling among the officers concerning the various items listed; and, regarding the second term: that the Americans could carry off all their belongings except their munitions of war, Washington was adamant in his refusal to sign.

"We would be better off as prisoners of war, than to attempt an unarmed march to the Potomac with scalp-mad savages after us. It would be suicide."

183

So Vanbraam had to make another trip back to Villiers and have the words *et munitions de guerre* stricken from the capitulation. When he returned the translation continued.

The final term demanded that the Americans must liberate and deliver the French prisoners taken at Jumonville's Glen. Until such a time when these prisoners could be returned to Fort Duquesne, Villiers demanded that two American captains be held by the French as hostages. Verbally, Villiers had requested that Vanbraam (because he spoke French) be one of these men.

Now the question was as to who the other officer would be.

It was understandable that none of the captains were in any great hurry to volunteer for this questionable duty; Hoag had a new wife awaiting him at home; Lewis was also a family man; and Murcer was the only officer in his company. Stephen had been promoted to the rank of major, and Mackay as a regular was not considered.

The Virginians looked askance at Robert Stobo.

The gentleman volunteer smiled blandly at Washington, and said:

"I would deem it an honor, sir, to become the volunteer hostage."

So it was agreed, and Vanbraam and Stobo signed their names in a blank space on the second page. Then Washington, with an unagitated hand, signed at the bottom, and Mackay as well—unintentionally, it would seem—scrawled his signature above Washington's.

The paper was then returned to the French and the business of capitulation was over. It was midnight.

Shad, Matt, Stefen and Stobo made a small fire outside the stockade and sat around it to talk. This was the last chance they would have to be with their friend for some time. It was even possible that they would never see him again.

"Why did you volunteer, Bobby?" Shad wondered. "You didn't have to. It's a risky business, you know."

Stobo seemed unconcerned over the risk. He looked at his three friends seriously.

"It's different with you three. You belong here because you were born here. It is enough, I feel, that you're willing to fight for your land. But I'm an outsider, an adopted son, and this country has been good to me, when it owed me nothing. Therefore, I must make an extra effort to pay my way."

He smiled at them.

"We'll meet again. But until we do, remember what I've told you: this land belongs to you; not to any crown, not to any foreign despot. Always be ready to fight for it. Never stop to reckon the cost or the odds. If they whip you today, come back at them tomorrow. Always be swift and audacious. *Celer et audax!*"

He paused to study them in turn; Stefen—small, quiet, determined; Matt—stalwart, open, intelligent; Shad—huge, brawling, independent as all get out. And he said, simply, "You can't lose."

In the morning the battered little army marched from Fort Necessity. The drum went *dddrum-ta-tum-ta-tum*. The shot-riddled Union Jack fluttered over their heads. They shouldered their muskets and drew one swivel gun after them, as agreed in the capitulation. Starving, beat from exhaustion and exposure, burdened with their sick and wounded, they stepped out with their heads up and their eyes straight ahead.

The French, drawn up in two long ranks before the fort, presented arms as the Virginians and regulars marched down the aisle. The Abenakis and Mingoes skulked along the sidelines casting surly glances at the unvanquished Americans.

Shad spotted Half King and his retinue of Senecas standing at the fringe of the woods, watching the retreat proceedings with wooden expressions, and he raised his musket and gave a shout.

"Hi-yi! Heads up! We're passing Tanacharison, the Terror of Jumonville's Glen, mates! *Salve,* great warrior chief of *ne Eia'dagen'tci!* Hail to the grammaw of the old women!"

Half King glowered with rage and shouted back at Shad in Seneca.

"The French have behaved like cowards, and the English like fools! I wash my hands of all white men!"

"Just your hands, old lady?" Shad bellowed. "How about the rest of you? It could sure use a washing!"

The Americans needed a laugh just then and Shad had handed them a dandy. They roared at Half King's expense. Then Matt noticed Harry Curry standing behind one of the French lines. He was quite alone and he was watching the passing army with an enigmatic expression on his pale, haggard face.

Slowly Harry turned away and walked over to where Vanbraam and Stobo were sitting together on a log. The Dutch and Scot soldiers of fortune glanced at him blankly, and then stood up without a word or sign and walked away side by side.

Harry didn't seem to know what to do with himself. He appeared to be at a loss. He stood there alone in the trampled weeds and looked at Fort Necessity. Then, heavily, he lowered his head and stared at the ground. He didn't look after the Americans again.

A large group of paint-streaked Abenakis were following the Virginians and regulars right into the woods. They carried their tomahawks in their hands and it was obvious from their manner that they meant to harass the retreating army.

Ward was in charge of the afterguard and he was growing jumpy, especially so when he began to detect signs of panic among his men as the Abenakis pressed closer and closer.

Suddenly a batch of savages let out a whoop and rushed among the soldiers to snatch the medicine chests from the Virginians, which they quickly destroyed with their hatchets, while another clump of them grabbed two of the walking-wounded and started to drag them away.

Like a thunderbolt out of nowhere Shad Holly, enormous, profane, fire-eyed, tore into them with a swinging tomahawk, backed up by a squad (of all people!) of Carolina riflemen. The Abenakis fell away from the great brawling madman in disorder, and the regulars pushed after them with their bayonets.

The wounded were retrieved, and Shad walked back all beefy and sweaty and high-spirited. His ex-enemies, the regulars, grinning all around him, patted him on the back and called him a "by grab good scrapper!" Shad beamed at them and handed one of them a tomahawk.

"Here, brother, you ain't got no souvenir. That there's a gen-u-wine Huron sachem's war hatchet. I took it off him myself yesterday, and I ort a know!"

The weary army toiled slowly up a gradual hill. Matt saw Washington standing by the side of the trail watching his men drag themselves by. He watched them with a look of wistful compassion. He hated the sight of suffering, and he hated losing.

When Matt and Stefen approached him, he nodded through a break in the trees and, turning around, they could look back along a sloping ride of open land to the distant Great Meadows.

The little antlike figures of the Mingoes were trying to set the stockade on fire, yet still Fort Necessity resisted them. It was waterlogged with rain and refused to burn.

"I went out, was soundly beaten, and lost all," Wash-

187

ington said quietly. Then, after a somber moment, he raised his head and smiled at the two Pennsylvanians.

"Well, another day . . ." He turned and walked after his men.

Matt and Stefen watched him go. Matt said, "I've never felt so sorry for anyone in my life. After all he's suffered to make this expedition a success."

"Heck, he ain't whipped. You can't beat that man, Matt," Stefen said with conviction. "He didn't lose a war, just the first battle. And he only lost it by a slim margin. He'll be back. You'll see."

Matt put his hand on the hilt of the old claymore and felt a glow expand in his chest. Yes, Stefen was right: he would be back. They would all be back.

He watched the grim-faced fatigued army slog by him, and suddenly he knew that he loved these men, all of them. They were a new breed of men, born out of this sprawling fresh giant of a land. They were all Americans; even the regulars were provincials. And they admitted allegiance to no Crown, only to themselves.

There were cowards among them, some; and fools too; and some were hard-headed and heavy-handed; and many were as ignorant as dirt. You couldn't always like all of them all of the time, but you always had to admire them for their die-hard perseverance, for their deep-rooted lust for land and independence. They believed in their right to take what they saw spreading, growing, waiting before them, believed in it because of the burning-bright need in their souls for fertile earth and personal freedom.

What they saw, wanted, needed, they took; and they would give any encroacher a cold steely look which plainly said, This here's mine. Try to take it away from me and I'll flatten you. You might whip them today, but they'd be around again tomorrow and whip you back.

Urgent, eager, grabby, lusty, pushy, loudmouthed,

188

dangerous—they couldn't be anchored. They would be back again and again, and they would spread and sprawl in every direction because they knew what they wanted and there was no power on earth to stop them from getting it.

Then he saw Shad tramping gaily along. The big fellow was waving a deerskin pouch over his head, shouting, "Hi, Matty! Lookit what one a them regulars went and swapped me. It's a Abenaki *m'téoulin* bag and it's got no end a dandy magic gimcracks in it!"

Matt grinned at his huge friend, too exhilerated with his vivid picture of the Americans to answer. Then Shad paused and looked back.

"All right, Matty?" he called. "Ready to get on?"

Matt nodded and shouldered his musket and swung into the column of moving men. "Ready!" he said.

It was the fourth of July . . . and no one in that tired, tough little army could foresee what that date would one day mean to them, to their commander, and to their new-born nation.

REFERENCE

MONTCALM AND WOLFE by Francis Parkman, Little Brown and Co., 1897.

GEORGE WASHINGTON by Douglas Southall Freeman, Scribners, 1948.

HOUSEHOLD HISTORY OF U. S. by Benson J. Lossing, Chandler Bros., 1877.

UNCONQUERED by Neil H. Swanson, Doubleday, 1947.

FORT NECESSITY by Frederick Tilberg, Nat. Park Service *Historical Handbook,* Series No. 19, Washington, D. C., 1956.

TRAVELS OF GEORGE WASHINGTON by William Joseph Showalter, *National Geographic Magazine,* January, 1932.

WHERE WASHINGTON FIRST MADE HISTORY by Richard C. Underwood, *Together* Magazine, February, 1959.

The Author

When he left home at the age of sixteen, ROBERT EDMOND ALTER was determined that his career would be that of a social worker. At twenty, after working as a citrus picker and a score of other jobs that included being a movie extra, he found himself in the army. By the time he had reached his early thirties he was back to his youthful (earlier-than-sixteen) ambition of being a writer. He has had one adult novel published, as well as a novel for young people, THE DARK KEEP. In addition, he has written fiction for *Alfred Hitchcock's Mystery Magazine, Argosy, Boys' Life,* and *Saturday Evening Post.* Bob Alter lives with his wife and teen-age daughter in Altadena, California.